About the Author

Mannat Goyal (Age: 24 years) is an emerging writer in the Hindi literary world. She obtained a master's degree in Business Management from Amity University and is currently pursuing Ph.D. She has been among the Top 10 Fashion Influencers in Delhi and has gained tremendous popularity in the fashion industry at a very young age. She has also become an inspiration for millions on social media. Additionally, she is also an influential person and has experience as a presenter in a renowned news channel. She is a true lover of literature and has won several competitions in the field of writing. Since childhood, she has been deeply interested in Hindi literature and novel writing. The fictional roles created by her have the potential to inspire countless people.

AAKHIR Q

Mannat Goel

Contents

1

A Relationship of Compromise

One day, a call came from an unfamiliar number—strange, almost magical in its silence. When I answered, the voice on the other end wrapped around my heart like an old melody. It was hauntingly familiar. And in that fragile pause, Rehmat felt it in her heart that she had drifted so far into another world that even love, no matter how deep, could no longer bring her back… and he could never find his way to her again.

Mita kar likh rahi hoon, khatam jahan aakhir tak likha tha
Ki tere saath mera safar bas thoda sa likha tha.
Sab samajh gaye the, lekin tu kabhi nahi samjha,
Aur ab likh rahi hoon woh jo kabhi keh na saki main.
Ke tere jaane ke baad maine bandh kar diye woh saare darwaze,
Jin par teri dastak hoti thi… aur main guroor krti.
Tere baad meri in aankhon ne koi khwaab tak nahi dekha,
Yeh tha woh safar… jo tu kabhi samajh suku.
Mita kar likh rahi hoon, khatam jahan aakhir tak likha tha
Ki tere saath mera safar bas thoda sa likha tha.

Rehmat was a girl whose beauty felt like it had been borrowed from the stars. Her long, thick black hair flowed like midnight silk, and her eyes shimmered like diamonds under moonlight—capable of stopping time for anyone who met her. Draped often in white, she looked less like a girl and more like a dream in motion, a soft vision of an angel walking this earth. She wore her heart on her sleeve, feeling everything deeply, as if the world whispered directly to her soul. Though calm by nature, when Rehmat spoke, her words held the weight of poetry—measured, meaningful, and impossible to forget.

She dreamed of becoming an actress, of turning emotions into art, but her heart was so fragile that even the smallest slights could ignite her temper—because everything mattered to her. Her outer beauty was breathtaking, yes, but it was the tenderness of her heart that made her truly unforgettable. She had a quiet love for animals, a kindness so natural that even stray creatures seemed to trust her at first glance. She never wished harm on anyone and couldn't bear to see injustice—fighting battles even for those who might not have deserved her loyalty.

The world felt too loud for her gentle soul; even little things weighed heavily on her, and the bigger things, even more so. Perhaps that's why her world was small—just one true friend Aashna, her confidante since childhood. She rarely opened up to others—not because she couldn't— but because her presence was so radiant, people often admired her from a distance. She was tall, graceful, and impossible to miss. And when the wind played with her cascading hair, it was as if even nature paused to admire her. Rehmat wasn't just beautiful—she was the kind of girl who made beauty feel like something deeper than just a face… she made it feel like emotion.

It often happened with Rehmat that any boy she befriended would eventually fall in love with her, while other girls, envious of her beauty, preferred not to talk to her at all. In her life, there was no room for mistakes— once she turned away from someone, she never looked back.

"It's not important to have a hundred people in life; what truly matters is having that one person who surpasses all hundred."

She understood this lesson in a very short time. And the one person who had the strength to surpass those hundred was Aashna.

Rehmat had always witnessed her mother's hardworking life, where her mother toiled day and night to earn a living. To support her, Rehmat constantly came up with new ideas. She was obsessed with the dream of doing something great for her mother.Her mind danced far ahead of her years—wise, curious, and full of wonder— but the world only saw her youth, and in that innocence, they overlooked the brilliance blooming quietly within her.On the other hand, her mother's dream was to educate Rehmat. She wanted her to study well and build a bright future.However, Rehmat felt that studying and then achieving something in life would take too long—and she feared that in the meantime, her mother's health might deteriorate.

And by the time Rehmat achieved something, her mother might not even be in this world anymore.In reality, Rehmat's mother suffered from a mental illness that had no cure, and it was gradually worsening with time.

Her father had very little involvement in the household—his presence or absence hardly made a difference.She also had a much younger brother, who was only in the fifth grade.

The household expenses were managed entirely by her mother. Despite her illness, she never let herself become weak. She made every effort to keep herself fit and, in many ways, succeeded in doing so.No one could tell that Rehmat's mother suffered from a serious mental illness just by looking at her. When she spoke, her eyes moved as swiftly as a fish gliding through water, and her voice was so sharp that it felt as if it could pierce through ears. Her mind worked at such a rapid pace that she could find a solution to anything in the blink of an eye.She was a woman who stood firm in the face of every challenge, someone who had the passion to confront fear and defeat it with its own terror. Yet, as tough as she appeared on the outside, she was just as soft-hearted from inside.She was a woman who always called wrong as wrong and right as right—someone who could even consider the enemy of a friend as her ownand had the rare ability to follow her heart more than her mind.

While Rehmat's mother was handling the entire family and fighting against the odds to move forward, Rajeev had now entered in Rehmat's life.

Rajeev was even more handsome than Rehmat— he is tall, broad-shouldered, and strikingly attractive. He was a calm, innocent, and soft-hearted young man who spoke very little but was incredibly mature. Additionally, he was very wealthy.He was someone who minded his own business and was the eldest son of his family, deeply attached to his mother. Rajeev loved traveling and had a passion for trying new and exotic foods and why wouldn't he have such interests? After all, he came from a Punjabi family.At home, he had a sick mother who could no longer walk, an elderly father who had aged significantly, and a younger brother who was still studying. At an age when most hearts chase dreams, the weight of an entire household quietly found its place on Rajeev's young, fragile shoulders—turning his childhood into quiet strength. He worked as a Manager in a elite company.

During this time, Rajeev met Rehmat. Both were strikingly beautiful, and gradually, they became good friends. Their thoughts aligned in many ways, and as time passed, their friendship grew stronger.Now, they both of them started going everywhere together— eating, spending time, and sharing moments. Gradually, their families also came to know about their wonderful friendship.The best part was that Rajeev's family genuinely adored Rehmat and cared for her deeply. They took great care of even the smallest things related to her, treating her with love and affection.Seeing Rajeev's family's affection for Rehmat made her mother extremely happy. "Now, the worry surrounding in mother of Rehmat was gradually easing, perhaps because mother no longer had to look for a groom for Rehmat."

Both families were happy.

The rest of the story, in Rehmat's own words...

2

A Heartfelt Dilemma

But there was one person who was not happy at all that's me. I had countless questions and thoughts racing through my mind. My heart screamed something entirely different, but I couldn't say a word in front of my mother's happiness.I had lost to my mother's wishes, but I still had Rajeev—someone to whom I could open my heart.

One day, I gathered the courage to ask Rajeev to meet me.That day, my eyes were filled with tears, the usual glow on my face had faded, my hands were trembling, and it felt as if hot smoke was rising from my ears. Just then, I noticed Rajeev holding some food items in his hands. He placed them on the table and sat down on the chair right in front of me. The moment he sat down, I looked at him—and broke into tears.

Just then, Rajeev said, "Don't worry, everything will be fine."And without any hesitation, he started eating the food he had brought. Seeing all this, I was shocked. Now, I couldn't understand whether I should cry because I was deeply troubled inside or because Rajeev, my last hope, didn't even bother to ask me what was wrong. Accepting this reality was incredibly difficult for me. I was completely shattered from inside. For a moment, it felt as if I had lost my voice entirely. That day, on my way home, I kept thinking about this incident. I spent the entire night restless, unable to sleep, replaying that moment in my mind. I had now forgotten why I was initially upset—because Rajeev himself had become the reason for my distress. I couldn't understand why, but I simply couldn't let go of what he had done.

A few days passed in this inner dilemma. From that very day, a sense of bitterness had settled in my heart toward Rajeev. Maybe this wasn't such a big issue, but for some reason, it was eating me up from inside every single day. I started feeling that if he couldn't even bother to ask me why I was upset today, then tomorrow, he might never stand by me in my happiness or sorrow.

I picked up the pieces of myself and tried to forget… like it never happened.

Now, I found myself back at the same point—where I was supposed to tell Rajeev what was on my mind. But now, I no longer felt it was necessary to share it with him. After considering this issue, I decided to talk to my mother about it. The truth was that before getting married, I wanted to stand on my own feet and do something good for my family. I decided that I would go abroad from India and do something where I could earn more money and be happy, and after some time, bring my family along with me. My mother had already seen the spark—the silent longing to go abroad—glowing in my eyes. And for her, nothing else mattered more than the smile that dream brought to my face.

Now, the real challenge of my journey stood before me — and that was Rajeev. I didn't want to leave Rajeev midway, but on one side were my dreams, and on the other was Rajeev, waiting for me.I had to move forward, and in all of this, one thing had to be sacrificed. Choosing between the two became incredibly difficult for me. For days, I struggled with this inner dilemma every single day. Meanwhile, Rajeev, completely unaware of my uproar, was engrossed in his own life. He didn't care about anyone. He went to work, came home, ate, watched TV, and slept. It never even occurred to him that I was a part of his life too. Sometimes, I wouldn't speak to Rajeev for two whole days, and he wouldn't even notice. Despite everything even after all this, I **did not want to leave Rajeev alone**, because I wanted to leave this relationship on a **beautiful closure**. But Raaziv's attitude towards me no longer felt good at all. I didn't like it at all anymore.

I had started to find this world very ugly. After enduring a lot of difficulties, I decided to meet Raaziv and talk to him about it. Once again, I called Raaziv. I didn't want to keep him in the dark. Once again, my eyes were filled with tears. That day too, I hadn't come to leave him stranded midway; instead, I had brought along a solution that would resolve all my troubles. I told Raaziv everything—that I wanted to stand on my own feet, and this would only be possible if I left India and moved to Canada. But while holding Raaziv's hand, I asked, "Will you come with me?"

Rajeev couldn't understand what I was saying for a while, but when he saw tears in my eyes, he agreed to come with me. It felt like a dream to me—everything I wished for was coming true. My happiness knew no bounds. Just a heartbeat ago, the world wore shadows and thorns, but now, in a blink, it blooms in colors I'd never seen before.

3

Game

After some time, my college also started. I wanted to go to Canada on a study visa, and Rajeev had a very good connection with a company there, which is why he was getting a work visa. On one hand, I was quickly finishing my college studies, and on the other hand, Rajeev was preparing to leave everything and go to Canada for my sake. We were both very happy, and in all these things, almost eight months had passed. Whenever I would come back from college, the first thing I would do was meet Rajeev and tell him about my dreams every day, and then I would feel very happy. During that time, I felt like I was on top of the world.

They say that the faster someone climbs up, time throws them down twice as fast.

This is something similar that happened to me. It had been almost ten months, and I wanted Rajeev to go to Canada before me because I still had two years left in my college. But I never got any response from Rajeev. Whenever I talked to Rajeev about Canada, his only response was, "The process is going on, I have applied, just waiting for the email." Every day, I would pray to God, hoping Rajeev's email would come, and then I could fulfill my life's dreams. One day, I cried in front of Rajeev, saying, "I don't know when Rajeev's visa email will come, I don't know why God is making me wait so long. I've been so troubled and frustrated, and for this email, I've been feeling so anxious." Rajeev's only response to all of this was, "The process is going on, just waiting for the email."A few more days passed with the same patience. One day, Rajeev was sitting with me, talking, and then he left his phone behind to attend to something. I kept looking at Rajeev's phone intently, and for some reason, I suddenly decided to pick it up. With great curiosity, I started searching for the visa application Rajeev had sent. I tried very carefully to find that application, but no matter what, after searching for a long time, I couldn't find it. Seeing this, I started feeling restless, and I ran to Rajeev. In a low voice, I asked him, "Why haven't you sent the application yet?" Hearing this, Rajeev was completely shocked. He couldn't understand what was happening all of a sudden. Before he could even explain himself, I became furious with him. Now, Rajeev had no choice but to tell the truth.

(Rajeev said – I haven't applied yet because I don't want to go to Canada. I am very happy in my own country, and moreover, I can't leave my parents. As soon as Rajeev said this, Rehmat broke down in front of him and started crying uncontrollably. Once again, Rehmat's dreams were shattered. She couldn't even compose herself. She couldn't believe that this was the same Rajeev who had been so devoted to her. A whole year of Rehmat's life had been wasted. The whole world suddenly seemed bad to her again. Seeing this, Rajeev felt sorry the next day and tried to console Rehmat, explaining that he couldn't leave his family.)

But I don't know why, I always felt that I wouldn't find anyone better than him in the whole world. He was rich, handsome, had a great way of talking, and the biggest thing was that I never had a fight with him. I had never seen him angry, and whatever care he showed me, it always felt like too much. Maybe it was because he was the first person in my life like this. Before him, I had never formed any kind of friendship with anyone.

Rajeev's decision not to go to Canada shattered my love, dreams, and career. I was heartbroken because now I couldn't go to Canada without Rajeev. I had to either let go of Rajeev or my dreams, but the harsh truth was that I had to sacrifice one of them.

For many days, I sat in silence, lost and uncertain, unsure of whom to trust—but slowly, I gathered the scattered pieces of myself, and with time, Rajeev began to fade from the chambers of my heart; our conversations grew rare, our meetings rarer still, and now, even his words, once dear, began to weigh heavily on me.

(For example, whenever they went out to eat, whatever the bill was, on Rajeev's suggestion, Rehmat would pay half, and Rajeev would pay the other half. Sometimes, Rehmat would think, "How can such a rich man not even be able to cover her food expenses after marriage?" However, Rehmat didn't like to travel much, nor did she ever spend much on anything with Rajeev. In fact, whenever she went anywhere, she always bought everything with her own money. He had become less of her fiance and more of an ordinary person to her.)

But Rajeev's habit of splitting everything in half had broken me in half. I started distancing myself from him on my own. Sometimes he shattered my dreams, sometimes he gave me false assurances, and sometimes he even kept track of our food expenses. All these things were making me stronger day by day.

On the other hand, Rajeev was also busy with his own life. He didn't care about my feelings or whether I talked to him or not. Meanwhile, I was also trying to pull myself together. I no longer wanted to be trapped in this web of lies. As time passed, Rajeev's place in my heart gradually faded into nothingness. Eventually, I told him that there was no passion left in our relationship and that it would be better for both of us to go our separate ways. I wanted to say many things to him, but before I could, Rajeev simply replied, "Alright."

Hearing his **"Alright"** made me realize that he had just been waiting for me to break-up. Otherwise, a person who truly loves would at least ask why I was ending the relationship. It felt as if he had been eagerly waiting for this relationship to end.

4

A Quiet Entangled Feeling

Now, I was focusing on myself and spending day and night dreaming about going to Canada. But then, I would feel disheartened and sit alone in my room in silence.

> *"Mera dil khushi chahta tha*
> *Mann sambhalna chahta tha*
> *Samjhdari kmana chathi thi*
> *Aur main yeh sab kuchh*
> *Eak shakhs ke pichhe haar baithi thi"*

Carrying so many buried emotions in my heart, I would wake up every day and go to college, but I no longer felt connected to it. Going to college had become a compulsion for me, something I just wanted to finish as soon as possible. My heart and mind were constantly troubled beyond limits. Thinking about all these things, I fell into depression and developed migraines, which caused my head to ache all the time. The pain was so intense that I had to tie a cloth tightly around my head while going to college. Pain had settled in both my head and my heart. Months passed like this, but eventually, I pulled myself together. I no longer needed anyone. I had made myself strong.

5

My Moon

---♡---

"They say that before something great happens, a lot of bad things take place."

This is the truth-----

There was a show at my college—a modeling show. Feeling hopeless about life, I don't know what came over me, but I decided to participate in it. Just a few days after joining, I became the lead model for the show.For the first time in months, I felt a little happy. The show was scheduled for 7 PM. We all put our hearts into it, and I got so immersed in the performance that I didn't even realize when it had already turned 9 PM.

For me, going home alone at this hour was not safe. Still, I called home, but my father wasn't there. That's when my friend, Ameesha, suggested that I shouldn't take the risk of traveling alone so late at night and should stay at her place for the night.

I called at home and informed them that I would be staying at Ameesha's place for the night. My mother didn't object because it was safer for me to stay at Ameesha's house rather than coming home late at night. For the first time, I was going to stay over at a friend's house.

(Rehmat's decision that night was about to change her life forever. She had no idea what was about to happen to her. Unaware of everything, she happily went to Ameesha's house. The two of them were sitting in the room, chatting, when suddenly, the doorbell rang—only a few seconds stood between Rehmat and a complete turn in her life.)

Just then, someone slowly pushed open the door to the room. I lifted my gaze and saw someone standing there. Half of his face was visible, while the other half was obscured by the dim lighting in the room. He was wearing a light gray shirt and black pants. Even in the low light, his eyes shimmered, holding an inexplicable allure—as if a layer of diamonds encircled them. His nose was perfectly straight, like a flowing waterfall, and his lips—there were no words to describe them. They sat on his face as if two rose petals had been placed on a cup of intoxicating milk. It felt as if the words that would emerge from them would be equally mesmerizing. I had never felt this way looking at anyone before, but his eyes… his eyes had already begun speaking to me.

He seemed slightly nervous and stepped forward to say "Hello" to me. I stood there thinking for a moment, unable to figure out who this person was. Just then, Ameesha came over and said, "He is both my friend and like a brother to me. He studies at our college too, but his course is different." When you find out that someone is from the same college, there's a natural sense of familiarity that makes you feel a little more comfortable. And that's exactly what happened to me.

Ameesha's room had nothing in it except a bed. The guy and Ameesha sat down on the bed. His legs hung off the edge, with half his body resting on the bed, supported by his elbow. Ameesha and he started talking to each other, but I had no interest in their conversation. He was casually scrolling through his phone when, suddenly, he mentioned Canada. The moment I heard "Canada," it was as if a surge of electricity ran through me. That was the first time I asked for his name. He told me his name was Raaz. It was quite an unusual name—just as unique as he was.

I asked him when he was going to Canada, and he said, "In the next six months." I didn't show much interest in the topic, but deep inside, it felt like a small spark had been lit in the extinguished lamp of my heart. He was the first person whose phone number I had ever asked for myself, and without hesitation, he entered his number into my phone. Raaz had come with his friend, Gaurav. What I didn't know at the time was that Gaurav had liked me for a long time. Only Raaz was aware of this. As we kept talking, we didn't even realize when it had become 1 AM. Suddenly, Raaz had to leave for some work and stepped out. At that moment, Gaurav turned to me and said, "Come on, I want to take you somewhere."Hearing this, I immediately refused. After all, I had just met Gaurav for the first time, and going somewhere with a stranger at 1 AM felt risky. But he kept insisting. Even after a long time, I didn't agree—until Ameesha spoke up, "Come on, let's go. Don't worry, he's like my brother. It's really nice to go for a night drive." Ameesha reassured me, and only then I agree. The three of us got into the car and drove off. The entire road was surrounded by forests, stretching into the distance with no one in sight. A part of me felt anxious about going somewhere unfamiliar with Gaurav, but seeing Ameesha with me gave me some courage. Eventually, the car stopped at a cemetery. The place was eerily peaceful, almost soothing. There was a pond, and I could hear the gentle sound of water flowing. When I stepped out of the car, I felt an unexplainable sense of calm. There was something comforting about the place. After spending some time there, Gaurav suggested we leave. I wanted to stay a little longer, but I didn't say anything. We got back into the car and drove toward home. When we returned, we saw that Raaz was already there—waiting for me. Raaz immediately asked me, "Where did he take you?"I replied, "To the cemetery."

Raaz looked at my hair—they were long and left open. At that moment, he told me to tie them up. Then, he called Gaurav over and started scolding him harshly. His anger was justified—who takes two girls to a cemetery at 1 AM? This led to a heated argument between the two of them. For the first time, I felt a slight realization—this person genuinely cared. Even Rajeev had never shown this level of concern for me, yet Raaz, in our very first meeting, had done so.

It was 3 AM, and the four of us started playing a game. During the game, Ameesha gave me a dare—I had to do a couple's dance with Raaz. It was just a game, so I accepted the challenge.What I didn't realize at that moment was that the person whose hands were on my waist, whose eyes were locked with mine, would soon become more precious to me than my own life. Seeing all this, Gaurav couldn't control his anger. He suddenly stood up and said, "I'm leaving. I have work in the morning." I already understood what was going on in Gaurav's heart. I tried to stop him, but he left anyway. As soon as he left, Raaz also decided to go with him. I didn't want Raaz to leave at all, but I couldn't bring myself to say anything to stop him. In just a few hours of meeting him, I had already started to feel a strange sense of connection with him—as if he was already someone special to me.

The next day, I went to college, and suddenly, Raaz called me. Seeing his name on my phone, my eyes lit up with excitement. Raaz asked me to meet him and also told me to bring Ameesha along. The three of us met again at college, and after classes, we casually went out for a drive.

I was sitting in the front seat beside Raaz, while Ameesha sat in the back. That day, I realized just how well-known Raaz was throughout the entire college. With Raaz, it was as if every step he took, he was greeted by someone who knew him. Every corner of the college had people who not only knew him but also respected him. That day, he dropped me home, but before leaving, he also gave me his favorite chocolates. When I saw them, my eyes widened in shock—because it wasn't just one or two chocolates. It was around five thousand chocolates!

I had no idea what I would do with **so many chocolates**, but seeing them, **tears welled up in my eyes**—because **no one had ever done something like this for me before.**

Raaz wanted to become a political leader in life, and he had already adopted the demeanor of one. The way he spoke was incredibly captivating. He had a natural charisma, a power that could draw anyone toward him. There was something magnetic about him—he could make anyone fall under his influence in just two minutes. (*In his own words, he called this "getting someone into the bottle."*)

When he spoke, it wasn't just his words that communicated—his eyes spoke too. His way of speaking had the ability to turn even a sworn enemy into a brother in just a minute. As much as he was playful and resourceful, he was equally emotional and deep. There was nothing impossible for him—as if he had a magic wand that no one else knew about.

6

A Promise Till The End

Raaz was from Muzaffarnagar, but his parents never wanted him to become a political leader. Eventually, he gave in to their wishes and focused only on his studies, though his heart was never in it. Even in college, he couldn't resist getting involved in student politics, and by then, I had also become very close to his heart. But while Raaz loved being surrounded by people, I was completely the opposite. I never liked crowds or engaging in too many conversations. Being around too many people made me anxious. Raaz, however, believed that I would be impressed by his extensive network and influence—but he was wrong.

Sometimes, I would get overwhelmed by crowds. With time, Raaz realized that if he wanted to spend time with me, he needed a quiet place with no distractions. Day by day, I was getting closer to him. Whenever he wanted to meet me, he would clear out the entire college coffee shop, asking all the students to leave. I don't know if it was childishness or love, but every time he did this, I couldn't help but laugh to myself.

But as soon as we would sit there for a while, the coffee shop would become so silent that I wouldn't feel comfortable anymore. Then I would tell Raaz, "Let's go somewhere else."Seeing this, Raaz would get confused—he couldn't figure out what exactly I wanted. Poor Raaz had to guess my feelings and understand me without me saying much. Since I didn't like crowds, Raaz started meeting me in secret, avoiding people so that no one would stop him on the way for a conversation. But after some time, I started liking his friends and his fan following. Slowly, I stopped living my own life and began living in Raaz's world.

One day, I was sitting at Ameesha's house when suddenly Raaz arrived. Without saying a word, he grabbed my hand and led me toward the elevator. I started wondering, *"Is he about to do something wrong?"* My heart was racing with nervousness.Even though I had only known Raaz for a few days, this sudden moment made me anxious. Then, with a sudden jolt, the elevator stopped on the 21st floor. Now, we were standing at the very top of the building. The night was dark and deep, with the moon smiling down at me. Stars twinkled in the sky, and the cool

Made by - Mannat Goel

breeze ran through my hair, touching every strand. There was absolute silence all around. Looking down from that height, the world below seemed so small—for a moment, I felt like a princess. There was a strange sense of peace in that moment. When I turned around, I saw Raaz quietly gazing at me with eyes full of love.His eyes had a certain glow, and for some reason, looking into them made my heartbeat race even faster. The more I looked at him, the faster my heart pounded. I had an urge to hold him in my arms and make this peaceful moment unforgettable. But I didn't have the courage to even touch him. As we started descending from that great height, I was terrified. Sensing my fear, he extended his hand toward me, offering support. I didn't get his embrace, but at that moment, his hand was enough to chase away my fear. As soon as I held his hand, he started recording a video on his phone. He had a habit of capturing every little moment on camera.

Time was passing beautifully, and I was immensely happy with Raaz. Raaz treated me like a queen—if I called day as night, he would agree without question. He treated me like a little child, fulfilling all my small wishes. Every day, he made sure to drop me home from college. I don't know from whom he borrowed cars, but he always arranged one just to take me home, as if I were his responsibility. During those rides, he always played one particular song: *"Ek tu hi yaar mera, mujhko kya duniya se lena"* That song became etched into my soul.

I considered myself very lucky to have Raaz in my life. But sometimes, I wondered—Raaz is Muslim, and I am Hindu—what would happen to our relationship in the future? Still, no matter what, I believed that Raaz and I would always be together. Whenever I looked into Raaz's eyes, I could see nothing but love for me. Since Raaz lived away from his family, he often ate outside food, which I didn't like at all.

Sometimes, I would bring his favorite dal makhani and rice, sometimes vegetables and roti, and occasionally, I would give him his lunchbox early in the morning before heading to my class. Everything was going perfectly, and Raaz had taken Rajeev's place so completely that it felt as if Rajeev had never even been a part of my life.

That phase was **the most beautiful phase of my life**.

I kept making Raaz promise me the same thing again and again.

I used to say to Raaz,
'Promise me you'll stay with me till the very end.'
I said it with such depth and intensity that Raaz would pause,
compelled to wonder—what does 'till the very end' truly mean?
Then he'd smile, hold my hands gently in both of his, and say,
'I'll always be with you.'
I'd interrupt, 'Raaz, say till the very end,' and he'd laugh and reply,
'Yes, yes—I'll stay till the very end with my chapri.'

7

A Downpour of Misunderstandings

(Now, Rehmat was no longer just Rehmat for Raaz; she had become his Motu, Gudda, Chapri, his little baby! Raaz had also started visiting Rehmat's house. Their friendship had grown so deep that people had begun to feel jealous. Many tried to create misunderstandings between them, but Raaz and Rehmat were happy together. They ruled the entire college, and now Rehmat had also embraced Raaz's ways, joining him in his political endeavors.)

Raaz had now become my strength, and I had become Raaz's life. On the other hand, Rajeev had started feeling my absence; he would occasionally call me to check on me.

It was the time of Diwali, and for the first time, Raaz brought me a gift. He had brought a very beautiful gold ring. Seeing that ring, I was very happy because it was the first time someone had given me a ring. There was a heart engraved on the ring, which enhanced its beauty even more. But the very next moment, I became sad, thinking about how I could accept such an expensive ring. The next day, with love, I returned the ring to Raaz, but he felt very bad about it. This led to a big argument between us, but I refused to accept the ring.

One day, Raaz came to drop me home from college. As soon as I got out of the car, an acquaintance of Raaz happened to be there. Shortly after, I received a very angry call from Raaz, and he asked me…

"Who is Rajeev? And what is he to you?" Hearing this, I got a little nervous because I never wanted Raaz to find out about Rajeev. His next question was, "You were already with someone, so why did you play with my feelings?" Hearing this question, I felt the ground slip from beneath my feet because there was no truth in it. I explained to Raaz that there was nothing like that. Yes, it was true that Rajeev and I went to the same gym, but now I had no connection with Rajeev. Raaz was finding it hard to believe. I could clearly see the fear of losing me in his eyes.

Rajeev's presence had now become a part of both Raaz's and my life, even though he was no longer there. Perhaps it would have been better if I had told Raaz everything about Rajeev from the beginning. The way this matter was presented to Raaz was completely wrong. Things that were once filled with love were now turning into suspicion. Everything was going in the opposite direction. I don't know whose evil eye had affected us. For many days, Raaz's mind was filled with countless questions, while on the other hand, I kept explaining myself every day. This went on for months, and eventually, I stopped replying to Rajeev's messages altogether.

After a lot of explaining and enduring countless difficulties, I was trying to clear up all the misunderstandings. "I had so much to achieve in life, but then he came along, and my whole world became limited to him." But Rajeev was still like a thorn in Raaz's heart. He wanted to trust me, but he was helpless before his own heart. His doubts kept growing inside him, blinding him to everything else, including me.

Raaz became very disturbed about Rajeev because Rajeev was independent, he was good-looking, and most importantly, he was Hindu. On the other hand, Raaz had nothing to offer me except his love. These thoughts were tormenting Raaz from inside. Rajeev's qualities were slowly eroding Raaz's confidence, and he became deeply engrossed in his own mental and emotional struggles. Perhaps he was unaware that all I ever wanted from him in return was love. Even during this difficult time, when he had no money for outings, no car, no wealth—I still chose him. And I would always choose him. Raaz became so fearful of Rajeev that he even stopped me from going anywhere. What else could I do? I simply said,

"Tu mujh ko apni kaid me rakh, aag lge dunia ko"

But quitting the gym was very dangerous for my health because I had some medical conditions that could only be managed through exercise. However, Raaz was so consumed by his paranoia that he could see nothing beyond Rajeev—not even me, nor my health.

One day, during a conversation, he asked me where Rajeev lived. I told him that Rajeev lived in Krishna

Colony. As soon as Raaz heard this, he said, "Why are you lying to me? He doesn't live in Krishna Colony; he lives in Maura Vihar. And he doesn't have any grand mansion or a car either."

Hearing this, I was stunned—why had Rajeev lied to me so much? It wasn't about the small house or the car; it was about the lies. He had lied to me about everything. And to top it all off, I was about to marry a man whose home I didn't even know the real location of. First, he played with my emotions just to go to Canada, and then he lied about every single thing about himself. In that one moment, I completely removed Rajeev from my heart. I thanked God a thousand times that I had been saved from such a huge deception and that I learned the truth because of Raaz. However, I never mentioned this truth to my family.

Out of basic human courtesy, I used to respond to Rajeev whenever he reached out. Amidst all this, I found out that Raaz and Rajeev had already spoken to each other—something I had no idea about. In their conversation, Rajeev had told Raaz: "Why are you getting involved with her? Just use her and leave. And how did you even get her? Did you lure her with something? Money? Her body?" To this, Raaz responded sarcastically, "Yeah, brother, I showed her fancy cars and riches. I made a huge mistake."

When I found out about this, I was deeply hurt by how wrongly both of them thought about me. This was Raaz's first mistake, and it still pricks my heart to this day. As for Rajeev, there was no point in being upset with him—

what could be expected from a person who was trying to build a relationship based on lies? I never told Raaz about Rajeev because I knew Raaz wouldn't be able to handle the thought that my past could overshadow his love for me. I cared so much about Raaz that I forgot to consider what he thought of me. This was a significant matter, and I did bring it up with Raaz. He apologized to me for it, and eventually, I let it go.

As time passed, my health started deteriorating significantly. I began to look overweight and unappealing, like an old lady. I was constantly in pain and felt irritable all the time, which led to many terrible fights with Raaz. During those fights, I would often say hurtful things to him. I don't know what he was made of, but despite everything I said, he never used a single harsh word against me. To him, even my worst traits seemed beautiful. And why wouldn't they? After all, he always called me his love. This was one of Raaz's most admirable qualities.

8

The Pandemic

Raaz and I used to have intense fights, but no matter what, we always ended up together. He couldn't find peace without me, and for me, everything began and ended with him. I had gotten used to living in a golden cage—golden because it was built with Raaz's immense love. As for money, I was certain that if I was standing by him during his tough times, then his good times would also belong to me.

There came a time in Raaz's life when he even left his family behind just for me. It was the year 2020 when the entire world was in chaos due to COVID-19. A lockdown was imposed. People were rushing back to their villages.

On the other hand, Raaz was restless, wondering how he would meet me now. His mind wasn't occupied with thoughts of his mother, sister, or father—he was only thinking, with his mischievous mind, about how he could live without seeing me. That day, he was very anxious, and so he called two of his friends, Shri and Utsav. Utsav was driving the car, and Shri was sitting in the front passenger seat. Raaz and I were in the back seat. Suddenly, Raaz gently laid me on his lap, placed his hands softly over mine, and seemed lost in his thoughts. His eyes spoke volumes to me that day. Then, all of a sudden, he started playing with my cheeks, just like a child plays with his favorite toy. He kept calling me sweet names—"Mera Gudda, Mera Chappu, Meri Chapri"—making me laugh endlessly. And amidst all this, I didn't even realize when we reached my home.

Due to the coronavirus, all the friends who used to stay with Raaz had returned to their homes. In the end, only one of his brother remained with Raaz—his name was Ahan. Ahan was the only son in his family and bore the entire responsibility of the household on his own. He was a very mature, hardworking, and quiet person. Over time, he became like an elder brother to me, and I lovingly called him "Bhai." Raaz and Ahan always stood by each other wholeheartedly. Although Ahan was older than Raaz, he would still fulfill even Raaz's unreasonable demands because of Raaz's persistence. They weren't real brothers by blood, but even if they had been, it was unlikely that a real brother would love Raaz as much as Ahan did.

A few days later, Ahan's family also started calling him back home because, during the coronavirus outbreak, everyone wanted to stay safe in their own homes. Even after Ahan tried to convince him countless times, Raaz didn't consider it necessary to go back home. After Ahan left, Raaz was very scared to sleep alone at night. For many days after Ahan returned home, Raaz couldn't sleep alone.

I started putting Raaz on a video call while sleeping. With the help of a small phone, he was now able to sleep. During the video call, he would talk a lot, and I had almost become like a child in front of him. Sometimes, I would dance like a cartoon for him, sometimes make funny faces like a clown, and sometimes scare him by pretending to be a ghost. There were even times when he got so scared that he would run out of his room in fear.

Those moments were the most memorable moments of our lives. Raaz was aware of it, but I had no idea. In just a few months of meeting, we had become like two hearts and one soul. Due to the pandemic, the college had closed for the holidays. With nothing else to do, we would talk all day long, and at night, we would fall asleep on a video call together.

9

All Yours

After some time, as the pandemic eased, we resumed meeting each other. Raaz would often borrow his friends' cars to come and see me. In return, he had to do a lot of favors for them and even agree to their unreasonable demands. Just for the sake of a car, he sometimes gave up his own room for his selfish friends and slept outside himself. He couldn't bring himself to leave those friends, all because of that one car.

I had been observing all of this for many days, and then a moment came when I couldn't tolerate it anymore. I had to get a car for Raaz, no matter what. I couldn't bear to see him bowing down to anyone. I was completely obsessed with the idea of getting him a car. Anyone who spoke or thought badly about Raaz—I distanced myself from them even before Raaz did. For me, Raaz's enemy became my sworn enemy.

At the age of twenty, I gathered money from here and there, withdrew some of my savings, borrowed some from my mother, and bought a second-hand car for Raaz. I handed him the keys. Raaz was happy, but not too happy because the car was old, and he was used to driving big, expensive cars. During that time, even though I wasn't earning, I did everything I could because he really needed a car. It wasn't that his family couldn't buy him a car, but because Raaz hadn't returned home during the COVID period, his family was very upset with him.

During that time, I decided to pursue my acting career. I had always wanted to act, and now that Raaz was with me, I knew I would be safe from the bad intentions of people because, in the acting industry, there are both good and bad people. To fulfill this dream, we both set out toward our goal. I started working on my own. Both of us would wake up at five in the morning and set out toward our destination.

(Sometimes, the scorching heat of the sun would directly strike them because they would shoot either by the roadside or in an empty field. It would take Rehmat about an hour for a single shoot, and they would usually do at least three shoots. During that time, Raaz would take care of Rehmat's bag, sometimes hold her phone, sometimes help her put on her slippers, and even cover the car with clothes so that Rehmat could change. Sometimes, Raaz would fall seriously ill because he couldn't tolerate the heat—he was more delicate in this matter than Rehmat. But seeing Rehmat, he never gave up. Rehmat was his strength, and he knew very well that if he faltered even a little, Rehmat would abandon everything. He never shared his pain or troubles.)

The effects of COVID were still lingering. Since he hadn't gone home, his family had stopped sending him money, which left him deeply troubled. That was the worst phase of his life—everyone had abandoned him, and because he had no money, no one even cared to check on him. When I found out about this, how could I just sit idly by? The very next day, without telling Raaz, I brought every little and big thing he might need. At that time, I just wanted to take care of him. I wasn't earning a single rupee, yet despite that, I put everything I had into supporting him. I asked Raaz, "Is there anything else you need?" Before he could answer, my eyes fell on the table. Raaz loved table lamps. He didn't have a kettle for hot water. He lacked enough mattresses and bedsheets for sleeping. Moreover, he really liked my favorite blanket and bedsheet—he had specifically asked me for them. That was the first time I hesitated about giving him something. But it was Raaz in front of me. How could a mere blanket hold any value compared to him? I picked it up, got it washed, packed it, and handed it to him. I didn't know why he wanted that blanket so much, but when he received it, Raaz was incredibly happy.

During Raaz's tough times, I always stood by him like his shadow. As much as I loved him, we fought twice as much. But there was never a day when Raaz let me go to sleep angry without making it up to me. Sometimes, he would even come to my house in the middle of the night just to console me, and then he would return home and fall asleep on a video call with me.

The COVID era was extremely painful for everyone. On the other hand, Raaz was also bravely facing every battle. It was the worst time for him—sometimes, he didn't even have money for daily expenses, and other times, he struggled with fuel for his vehicle. And I stood by him like

Made by - Mannat Goel

a strong tree. I considered his every sorrow as my own and had the strength to overcome every hardship for him.

It was evening. Raaz was lying in my lap. The rays of the setting sun were entering his room through the balcony, slowly descending beyond the horizon. There was complete tranquility all around, and flocks of birds were returning home. With his head resting in my lap, Raaz kept gazing at the sun, lost in thought. I gently ran my fingers through his hair as he spoke about life—about where we would be in the coming days, about how quickly we had grown up without even realizing it. "I wish we could turn back time," he sighed. "Rehmat, this sun, this peace, this very day, you, and this evening—I will never be able to forget this moment."

There came a time when Raaz, despite wanting to, couldn't eat his favorite food. So, I would order his favorite meals for him, along with food for his friends as well. From Raaz's table lamp to bedsheets, pillows, blankets, essential utensils, a mattress for his servant, his medicines, groceries for him and his friends—I took care of everything. I neatly organized his wardrobe, ensured the bathroom had slippers, a wiper, a broom, a mop, food, bathing essentials like soap and shampoo. I knew his likes and dislikes by heart. I even cared for his face, making sure he looked his best. And when his servant ran away, I was the one who cleaned his bathroom too.

Sometimes, I couldn't believe that this was the same girl who used to find it difficult to even lift a glass of water, and here she was, doing every single thing for her favorite man—things she never liked doing at all.

During this time, Raaz had nothing to give that girl in return except for his love for Rehmat. Who doesn't like going out, having fun, and enjoying life? That girl had many dreams, but during that period, she gathered them all and locked them away in a corner of her heart—just by looking at Raaz.

10

The Gift

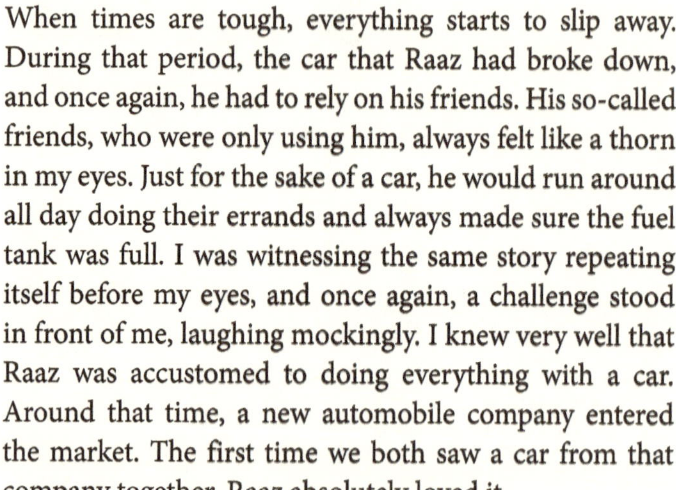

When times are tough, everything starts to slip away. During that period, the car that Raaz had broke down, and once again, he had to rely on his friends. His so-called friends, who were only using him, always felt like a thorn in my eyes. Just for the sake of a car, he would run around all day doing their errands and always made sure the fuel tank was full. I was witnessing the same story repeating itself before my eyes, and once again, a challenge stood in front of me, laughing mockingly. I knew very well that Raaz was accustomed to doing everything with a car. Around that time, a new automobile company entered the market. The first time we both saw a car from that company together, Raaz absolutely loved it.

That was it—I thought to myself, if a person could spend thousands on fuel, he could surely afford a car installment as well. Once again, I waited for the morning. I had one last chain with a locket around my neck and a delicate bangle—I sold them all. Selling those items gave me a few lakhs in hand. Now, the issue was the loan. At such a young age, I wasn't eligible for a loan. Somehow, after much effort and pulling some strings, I managed to make it happen, and finally, I got the loan. I wanted to give this car to Raaz as a birthday gift, but due to the loan process, his birthday passed, and the car arrived a month later.

And now, the keys to Raaz's favorite car were in my hands. Thank God that day he didn't like a car worth seventy to ninety lakhs, otherwise, I would have had to sell both my kidneys, my heart, and probably my eyes and bones too. After buying the car, I was completely drained. When I gave him the car, I had done everything I possibly could within my means. I couldn't celebrate his birthday with grand festivities, but yes, seeing the car made him incredibly happy. For quite a while, he couldn't even believe that it was actually his car.

(Now came the matter of the car's installments. Raaz and Rehmat made a decision that they would pay off the remaining installments together because the amount Raaz spent on fueling his friends' cars every month was actually less than what was needed for the car's installments. No one in Rehmat's family had the slightest clue about this car. On one side, Raaz stood by her with all his heart, and on the other, Rehmat stood for him with her heart, soul, and whatever little savings she had left. At that time, Rehmat wasn't earning a single penny. Just imagine, if she had been earning, then maybe the world would have had eight wonders—one of them being named after Raaz.)

Even after doing so much, there came a time when I could no longer manage Raaz's expenses. Everything was now stuck on give-and-take. Raaz was everything to me, and I wanted to help him at every moment, but whenever my mother asked for an account of the money, I could never provide an accurate answer. Somewhere, my mother was beginning to understand what was happening, but she pretended to be unaware despite seeing everything. At that time, I saw no one beyond Raaz. It wasn't that Raaz didn't return the money—he did, but sometimes not on time, which led to conflicts at home since my mother ran the household alone and entrusted me with the household expenses, which I often gave to Raaz when he needed it. During this period, an accident happened with my cat, and she passed away. Her death left me deeply disturbed and devastated. I was unable to take care of myself, let alone Raaz, so I advised him to go back to his home in Muzaffarnagar for a few days. Respecting my words, he chose to return to Muzaffarnagar.

11

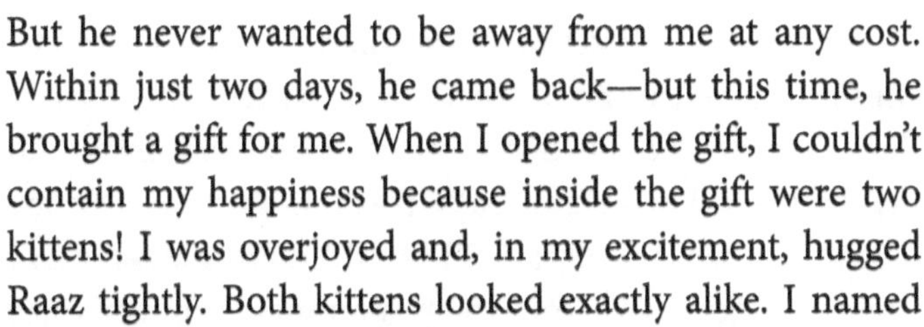

But he never wanted to be away from me at any cost. Within just two days, he came back—but this time, he brought a gift for me. When I opened the gift, I couldn't contain my happiness because inside the gift were two kittens! I was overjoyed and, in my excitement, hugged Raaz tightly. Both kittens looked exactly alike. I named one Kalo and the other Majju.

Along with the kittens, he brought another piece of good news for me—he told me that he wanted to open a small restaurant. Without wasting any time, we both started working on it. The restaurant had only two tables. It was small in size, but it carried a lot of my memories. I personally selected and bought every little thing for that place. That restaurant was a ray of hope for us. Through it, we wanted to overcome all our troubles and build something meaningful together.

It was the first day of the restaurant, and we were all very happy. I even brought a cake to celebrate. There were many people with Raaz that day, and when it was time to cut the cake, Raaz told me to step aside. I stood there silently for a while, lost in thought. When the cake was finally cut, I was standing at a distance, just watching

Raaz. I couldn't understand what had suddenly changed. Tears welled up in my eyes, and my heart slowly started to break. For the first time, I wasn't even a small part of such a big celebration in Raaz's life. On the other hand, my entire world revolved around him. Every part of me was shattering, while Raaz, for the first time, looked genuinely happy without me. This moment haunted me—I couldn't sleep peacefully for nearly nine nights.

This incident hurt me more than I could bear, and I couldn't keep it in my heart for long. Eventually, I asked Raaz why he did this to me. He had no clear answer to my question. For several days, this thought troubled me deeply. But what could I do? I loved him immensely, so I decided to let it go. From the restaurant's earnings, Raaz sometimes made a thousand rupees, and sometimes just seven hundred. But for me, this was worth millions—because it was earned by Raaz.

12

Red Rose

Some time passed, and Raaz wanted to buy a gold necklace for his mother. After putting in a lot of effort and careful thought, I selected a beautiful real pearl and gold set, keeping his mother's age and taste in mind. Raaz also liked it very much and gave it for making. On the other hand, I was also progressing in the acting industry, but I hadn't earned a single rupee yet.

Rehmat was so beautiful that she received major work opportunities every month—sometimes for a song, sometimes for a film. Everything would be finalized, but in the end, things would come to a halt for making some compromises. She would tell Raaz about it and cry a lot. Rehmat's dreams would suddenly soar to the heights of the sky, only to come crashing down face-first.

Raaz taking care of me like a child, encouraging me, and always standing by my side on one leg—somewhere, my mother had also started noticing all these things. Then came a day when my mother directly asked me if I wanted to marry Raaz. I replied with a "no," but my mother already knew what was in my heart.

(She sat Rehmat down beside her and lovingly said, "In life, you will find wealthy men, rich heirs, tall and handsome guys of every kind. But you should only choose the one who respects you and loves you like your mother does. The one who never lets you sleep without making up after a fight, who has the strength to stand up against the world for you, who accepts and hides all your flaws. And I see all these qualities in Raaz.")

The very next moment, tears welled up in my eyes, and my mother held my hand and said, "Look, don't be troubled. It doesn't matter to me whether he is Hindu or Muslim, nor do I care about what people will say. What matters to me is your happiness, and if your happiness is with Raaz, then so be it. Listen, my child, you will find many boys, one better than the other, but you will never find someone who loves you the way Raaz does. This boy travels all the way from Muzaffarnagar to Delhi just to make you smile, he can't bear to see tears in your eyes, he holds your every word with utmost respect, he cherishes you like a delicate flower. I like Raaz very much."

Hearing this, I couldn't believe that it was my mother saying all these things. Inside, I was going crazy with happiness. It was a joy filled with immense peace, a happiness that felt like it could erase every worry. I wanted to share this wonderful news with Raaz as soon as possible. But after thinking about it all night, I decided to keep it from him for now. One thought still pained me deeply—"Why did Raaz stop me from coming closer when he was cutting the cake that day?" That question kept shaking me from inside. And then, just a few days later, it was my birthday. I never liked celebrating my birthday because I always felt that whoever celebrated it would eventually drift far away from my life. But there was no way Raaz would let my birthday go uncelebrated.

At midnight, when the doorbell rang, I immediately knew it had to be Raaz. Raaz handed me a beautiful pink dress that he had specially bought for that day. I had always had a fear about my birthday—that whoever made me cut my birthday cake would eventually leave my life forever. I tried to explain this to Raaz, but he didn't understand. To him, my fear seemed meaningless.

The entire way, I kept thinking that if I cut the cake today, Raaz would leave me forever. A little while later, I started smelling roses from a distance, as if someone had created a whole garden of them. As soon as he opened the door to his house, I saw that the entire place was filled with red roses.

Under Rehmat's feet lay more than two lakh roses. Everywhere she looked, there were only red roses. Not a single wall of the house was visible. From the ground to the walls, everything was covered in red roses, their intoxicating fragrance filling the air. As Rehmat stepped forward, she saw that half of her college was present at her birthday celebration. She couldn't contain her happiness upon seeing everyone. When she looked up, she saw that the entire ceiling was covered with balloons—it wasn't just a ceiling anymore; it was a sky of balloons, each one adorned with a picture of Rehmat. The moment she saw all this, tears welled up in her eyes, and she stopped in her tracks. She knew that with every step she took forward, she would encounter something even grander. Truly, Raaz had put in immense effort for her birthday. Even in such difficult times, no one knew how he had managed to arrange all of this.

Raaz took my hand and led me to his room. He blindfolded me, and suddenly, an eerie silence filled the air. He reached toward my neck; I could clearly hear the sound of his breathing. Then, Raaz placed something around my neck. When I removed the blindfold, I was shocked—it was the same gold set that Raaz had gotten made for his mother.

(In reality, it was never for his mother—it was always meant for Rehmat. Seeing all this, Rehmat was overjoyed, and her happiness knew no bounds. She hugged Raaz tightly. They were both incredibly happy. Everyone stood in front of them, wishing Rehmat a happy birthday. The celebrations continued throughout the night with singing and dancing. By morning, everyone had returned to their homes. As Rehmat was about to leave, she hugged Raaz once again and said, "This necklace is too precious; I cannot keep it." Despite Rehmat refusing a hundred times, Raaz did not listen to her. He didn't let her take it off, insisting that it belonged to her and only her.)

Before leaving, I asked him one question: "Will you stay with me till the end?" He looked straight into my eyes and said, "Yes, my little crazy one, I will stay with you till the very end." Hearing this, I looked at him and smiled to myself. When I got home, I carefully placed all the gifts in my room. The whole night, I kept admiring them, feeling an overwhelming joy in my heart. I couldn't contain my happiness. I kept thinking over and over again—what good deeds had I done to deserve someone like Raaz? In just one day, we had created so many beautiful memories.

13

Destruction

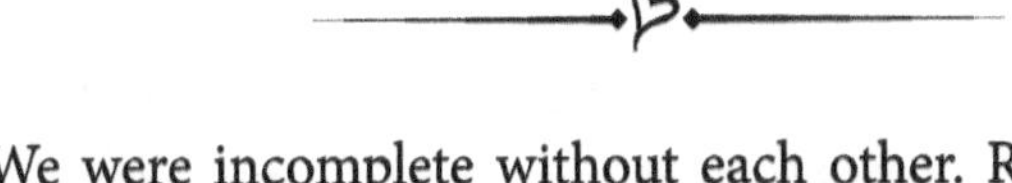

We were incomplete without each other. Raaz wouldn't do anything without me, and I wouldn't even step out of the house without him. And since there was so much love, it was obvious that there were a lot of fights too. I would argue with Raaz like a child, and he would always calm me down like one. But then, a time came when one small fight escalated so much that it created a huge rift between our hearts. In his anger, Raaz said something that shocked me—"Give me back my necklace, the one I gave you on your birthday." Hearing this, I felt really strange. Without any delay, I returned the necklace to him, and he took it back without hesitation. I couldn't understand why Raaz did that. We had fought thousands of times before, but never in any of those fights had we ever talked about taking things back from each other.

On one hand, I had sacrificed everything for Raaz, and on the other hand, Raaz had risked everything for just one or two lakh rupees. Once again, I felt like the ground had been pulled from under me. That necklace had held a special place in my heart—not because it was made of gold, but because it was something that would have stayed with me forever, something that would never deteriorate. Even if it had been made of clay, I would have still kept it safe for a lifetime. It would have remained precious to me, and perhaps I would never have even worn it because it was too valuable in my eyes. And so, I never asked for the necklace back. My heart was deeply troubled by this. This incident ruined many things between Raaz and me. Some time later, Raaz came to make amends, and along with that, he told me that he had sold the necklace.

Rehmat had never expected that Raaz would do something like this. Hearing this, she felt even worse—perhaps worse than she had ever felt before. She had never prioritized money over Raaz. She didn't know how to express love in words, but she always cherished him above everything else. But this was only the beginning. Rehmat still met Raaz every day, but their meetings no longer felt the same. The laughter, the spark, the joy, the mornings, the evenings, the streets—everything had become dull and lifeless. Their relationship had soured, though Raaz still didn't realize it. Rehmat was constantly angry now, ate her meals as if she had been starving for years, and would break into tears over the smallest things. Her mother could no longer bear to see her in this state, and one day, she finally asked Rehmat what was wrong. No matter how much Rehmat tried to hold herself together, she needed someone to ask her how she was. So, she finally told her mother the entire story of her birthday. Hearing this, her mother was deeply upset with Raaz because she had started seeing him as Rehmat's everything. But Raaz's small-minded actions had now created obstacles for himself. A mother is a mother—she would do anything to ease her daughter's pain. The very next day, she placed the same necklace in Rehmat's hands because Rehmat had cried over it all night. And if Rehmat had wanted five hundred such necklaces, her mother would have brought her five hundred of them, because she loved Rehmat even more than her own biological children. In truth, the bond between mother and daughter was incredibly deep—perhaps because Rehmat was not her biological daughter, and her mother never wanted Rehmat to feel like she didn't belong to this family. That's why, in both sorrow and joy, they always stood together. But even after receiving the necklace back, Rehmat didn't feel the happiness she once did.

After everything that had happened, my mother completely declared him worthless. According to her, if a man could make a girl cry so much even before marriage—and not only that but also sell off her birthday gift instead of realizing his mistake—then what would he do after marriage? I had always left every major decision of my life to my mother, and this time too, I chose to trust her judgment. After all these events, I had become extremely disheartened and distressed about Raaz. My mother could see my condition, and then, suddenly, one day, she placed my hand directly in Rajeev's. I had no other path left. I had removed Rajeev from my heart a long time ago, and now, making space for him again felt almost impossible. But still, closing my eyes, I chose to honor my mother's wishes.

(Rajeev was still waiting for Rehmat, and her return was a big victory for him.)

I was helpless. I couldn't leave Raaz, nor could I bring Rajeev into my life. My behavior was changing, which

Raaz couldn't tolerate. Some time later, Raaz found out about Rajeev because I didn't have the courage to tell him the truth myself. My choice was Raaz, but my compulsion became Rajeev. And then, once again, Rajeev came face to face with Raaz.

Raaz: Since when have you been talking to Rehmat?

Rajeev: We've been talking for about a year.

Hearing this, countless questions arose in Raaz's mind, and why wouldn't they? Deceiving someone for a whole year is a huge betrayal. He felt like everything I had ever done with him was just a pretense of love. Every word, every action, every concern, every bit of love—everything was a lie. I don't know why, but Raaz never even asked me once what the truth was. And asking was out of the question—

"Meri to ankhon me wo,
Neendo me wo,
Yaado me wo,
Khwabo me wo,
Wo ek shaks hai meri har baat me
Wo hai mere din me meri raat me,
Wo meri subah me meri shamo me,
Wo meri so soch me mere har ek kaam me,
Are mere liye to pana bhi wo aur khona bhi vo,
Mere liye hasna bhi wo, rona bhi wo aur jagna sona bhi wo,
Main jau kahi, main dekhu kahi
Wo hai waha, wo hai ha wahi,
Are kaise btau main use, uske bin to main kuch bhi nai,
Kahi bhi nahi..........

14

Conspiracy

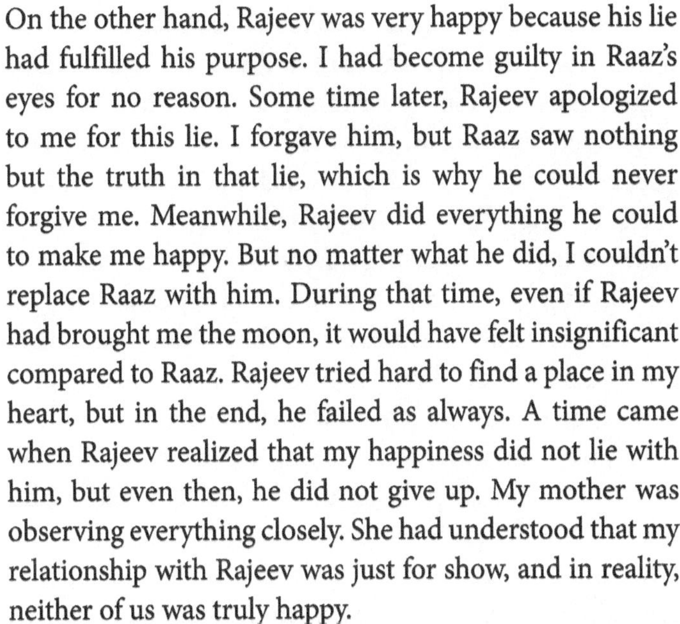

On the other hand, Rajeev was very happy because his lie had fulfilled his purpose. I had become guilty in Raaz's eyes for no reason. Some time later, Rajeev apologized to me for this lie. I forgave him, but Raaz saw nothing but the truth in that lie, which is why he could never forgive me. Meanwhile, Rajeev did everything he could to make me happy. But no matter what he did, I couldn't replace Raaz with him. During that time, even if Rajeev had brought me the moon, it would have felt insignificant compared to Raaz. Rajeev tried hard to find a place in my heart, but in the end, he failed as always. A time came when Rajeev realized that my happiness did not lie with him, but even then, he did not give up. My mother was observing everything closely. She had understood that my relationship with Rajeev was just for show, and in reality, neither of us was truly happy.

My relationship with Raaz had deteriorated significantly, but my heart was still deeply attached to him. I wanted to leave him because of his actions, but I was helpless in front of my own emotions. I was trying to balance both my happiness and my mother's happiness. But a person cannot sail in two boats at the same time. One of these boats was bound to sink, and that was Rajeev's boat. Rajeev had realized that neither would I step back on my own, nor would I ever truly be his. After witnessing everything, Rajeev himself decided to step away.

I no longer had anyone by my side from the heart. Raaz was clouded by misunderstandings, and I had driven Rajeev away with my own actions. I had become completely alone. Whenever I looked at Raaz, he always looked at me with suspicion. Sometimes, in his anger, he would lose his mental balance to such an extent that it became extremely difficult for me to handle. Our arguments often took place in the car, and while he never responded with words, he would drive so recklessly that people around us would start watching. Sitting with him when he was angry felt like brushing against death. He believed that I was playing a game with him or that I was taking revenge for my own loss. One of my flaws was that I never knew how to express love. I knew how to stand my ground, but I didn't know how to communicate properly. The biggest thing was that I was still learning from him what love truly was. But Raaz was incredibly stubborn— he would think about the same things day and night, which led to frequent clashes between us. And then, one day, I finally asked Rajeev why he had lied to Raaz. Rajeev replied, "For me, your respect is important. If anyone asks me whether you were with me or not, I will always say that you were, you are, and you will always be with me. Even if it's just as a friend, I will never let anyone make a mockery of this."

I couldn't understand whether Rajeev's actions were his greatness, love, or a conspiracy. Despite my countless attempts to explain, Raaz could never trust my character.

Rajeev's one statement had deeply wounded Raaz's heart—a wound that no healer could cure. Months passed in the same way. The fights and misunderstandings between Raaz and me had not yet been resolved, leading to my own mental distress. I began shouting over small matters, using harsh words, which started affecting the atmosphere at home as well. Raaz would ask me the same questions every day, repeatedly calling me unfaithful and a traitor. Eventually, a point came in my life where I started accepting every mistake as my own—because being wrong seemed easier than proving myself right. And so, accepting every fault as mine, I surrendered before Raaz. For me, my love was more important than my self-respect. That was my biggest mistake, because the Raaz who once loved me had now started making vile accusations against me. He had stopped believing in me. Raaz often talked about leaving, but I ignored those conversations because I trusted him more than I trusted myself. No matter how much he fought with me or how many hurtful things he said, he was still my Raaz—I believed he could never truly leave me. Even though Rajeev's presence had left a deep impact on our relationship, reducing the communication between Raaz and me, I still held onto the hope that Raaz would always be there.

(Raaz shattered that illusion as well. One day, he was taunting Rehmat about Rajeev, and that day, Rehmat thought that a person who repeatedly questions her character and never believes a word she says would probably call her characterless for the rest of her life.)

I didn't talk to him for a week, thinking that he would realize his mistakes. It seemed impossible that he could go a whole week without talking to me. But that, too, was my misconception—he managed to stay away for a week without reaching out. This was the same Raaz who once wouldn't leave without making amends whenever I was upset. About a week passed, and Raaz came to my house, ringing the doorbell multiple times. I was furious with him because now it felt like everything he did was just an act. Everything about him had changed. In his eyes, I was no longer good enough. He believed that I only gave him my car because it benefited me, that I had never done anything for him, that my love was just a facade. Now, even my question about the necklace was bothering him. To him, loving him, caring for him—it was all a conspiracy. He thought I was never there for him during his bad times, that I had only used him when he was struggling (at least, that's what he believed). I wanted to ask him just one thing—how could a girl possibly use someone who was already struggling financially? I had never made a single demand from him. I never went shopping with him, never watched a movie with him, never even accepted a gift. I walked alongside him every step of the way. Back then, I was still beautiful, I lacked nothing, and if I wanted, I could have had anyone with just a snap of my fingers. But I only wanted to fight with Raaz, to stay with Raaz, and, in the end, to spend my whole life with him.

(She could never say all this to him.)

I was extremely upset about all these things, and then he didn't even try to console me. He just rang the doorbell three or four times and then left that day, leaving me to my own fate.

15

Chameleon

(Two days later, a call came from a very strange number. It looked quite unusual. When Rehmat answered the call, the voice on the other end sounded very familiar. After a few seconds, she realized with certainty that this person had now gone so far away that even if she wanted to, she could never reach him again, nor could he come back to her. Hearing the voice, Rehmat was stunned. She couldn't comprehend what Raaz had done because the number was from Canada. It felt as if the ground had slipped from beneath her feet, and in an instant, her entire world had collapsed. It was as if someone had snatched away her whole universe. Raaz's happiness showed that he was on cloud nine, while Rehmat's tears had now settled deep within her eyes, with no bounds to their depth. She simply couldn't believe that Raaz had left India. Up until an hour before, she was still convinced that Raaz would never leave her behind. But Rehmat didn't let Raaz feel her pain. For a few days, they continued to talk over the phone. Sometimes, when Raaz had trouble cooking, Rehmat would guide him through video calls. There is a saying that when a blind man learns to walk, the first thing he does is throw away the stick that supported him. In this case, Rehmat had become that stick. One day, Rehmat saw some pictures of Raaz with foreign women, standing quite close to them. At first, he would post pictures once a month, but suddenly, he started posting many pictures every week. Seeing this made Rehmat restless because Raaz had never posted a single picture with her. And now, the place that once belonged to Rehmat was being given to someone else. Raaz had no idea what Rehmat was going through. Every time she looked at him, she would break down in tears. She couldn't believe that this was the same Raaz for whom she had sacrificed everything—her small joys, because Raaz never had the money to fulfill them. She never asked Raaz to take her anywhere, and shopping or watching movies were out of the question. This was the same Raaz for whom she never hesitated to do anything, whether it was two in the morning or three. She stood by him through every hardship and pain. And yes, this was the same Raaz for whom Rehmat had sold her childhood jewelry to buy him a car—just because she couldn't bear to see him begging from others. This was the same Raaz for whom she would fight anyone, no matter who they were. If someone was Raaz's enemy, they automatically became Rehmat's biggest foe. She might have had arguments with Raaz, but no one dared say anything against him in her presence. And yes, this was the same Raaz whom she had loved deeply.)

Now was the time for freedom, but I had fallen in love with the cage that Raaz had built. After Raaz left for Canada, I felt incredibly lonely because I finally realized that the world I had made around Raaz was never really mine to begin with. In my pursuit of Raaz, I had unknowingly left so many people stranded along the way. Now, I had no one left except for my friend Aashna. I shared all my sorrows and troubles with her, and she would stay up all night comforting and advising me. Being away from Raaz, I couldn't focus on anything. I was afraid to step out of the house alone, so I stopped going out altogether. I even left acting completely. Seeing me fall apart like this, my mother became my support and started taking me out. Though I slowly overcame my fear of the world, I still hadn't taken a single step forward after Raaz left—or perhaps, I still felt that my world was incomplete without him. While Raaz was living his life in luxury, I was fighting with myself every day and every night. I had two choices: either move on with my life or go back into his world and face more humiliation. And when, despite all his cruelty, I still couldn't let go of him, I finally spoke to Raaz one day. I told him that I wanted to come to Canada too. Hearing this, there was a flicker of happiness on Raaz's face, but deep down, he wasn't truly happy.

16

Worth

------◆♡◆------

(Mother knew that Rehmat's happiness was only with Raaz, and she, too, was growing weary of trying to console her. So, mother gave her permission. And with that, Rehmat began preparing for her paperwork.)

(During this time, I spoke to Raaz very little, and whenever we did talk, it turned into a fight. He came back to India for a few days, and over a small argument, things escalated so much that he questioned my worth and even my character. He told me that I had no status to go to Canada and threatened my entire family, saying he would tell everyone that 'I had ruined the life of a Muslim boy', that 'I had given him a car, and that I had used him like a driver'. It was around eleven at night, and he was standing in front of my whole family, openly declaring that he would create a scene in the entire neighborhood. That was the first time I realized I had made a huge mistake— he had stooped to such a low level. Before he could return and cause more chaos, my mother went to the police station and filed a complaint against him. While the complaint was being filed, my hands and feet trembled because I knew this was the final step—the last chapter of my journey with Raaz. After this, everything would end. I wasn't ready to let him go. My heart screamed for everything to be fixed somehow, but Raaz's anger was uncontrollable, and eventually, things came to an end. No one in my family wanted me to withdraw the complaint, but I insisted and somehow managed to take it back—because if I hadn't, he wouldn't have been able to return to Canada. Even after everything, I still thought about him.)

(In a single moment, everything was over. Within just a few hours, we had become strangers. I couldn't comprehend what had happened. One moment, I was preparing to go to Canada, and the next, my mind had completely stopped functioning. My entire world had collapsed. A few days passed, and I decided to continue with my preparations for Canada because, perhaps, I was yet to fall even further. With full determination, I took my exam for Canada, and I was confident that I would pass. But I failed by just a few marks. First, Raaz had left me, and now, it seemed even God didn't want to support me. But still, I didn't give up. I started preparing once again. I didn't even know why I still wanted to go there.)

Rehmat put in day and night preparing for the exam, but unfortunately, she missed passing by just a few marks for the second time. Despite this, she did not give up. During this time, there was nothing left between Raaz and Rehmat, yet somewhere deep inside, Rehmat still missed Raaz and kept questioning why he had said such a big thing. It was just a small fight that could have been resolved. Even after everything, she went to Chandigarh to take the exam for the third time. During this period, Raaz once again knocked on the door of her life. His love had returned. Raaz's return gave her immense courage. Once again, everything seemed fine; once again, his face became her strength. However, this only lasted for a few days. Before the results were announced, Raaz blocked Rehmat from everywhere. Then came the result day, and once again, Rehmat failed—this time by just half a mark. She broke down into tears because, until now, she had always gotten everything she wanted with determination. But for some reason, this exam of fate kept testing her over and over again. Defeated, she called Raaz, knowing that only he could console her in this tough time. But the moment Raaz picked up the call, he lashed out at her. In an angry and harsh tone, he told her, "Never call me again. I never want to talk to you." His words shattered Rehmat's heart into a thousand pieces. After all, she was leaving her home, her family, her country—everything— for Raaz. She never expected that he would speak to her this way. After this, her courage broke. She locked herself in her room. She stopped meeting people, stopped talking to anyone. She abandoned her acting shoots, her millions of followers—everything.

Raaz was only treating her as a pastime, while on the other hand, Rehmat's entire life depended on him. For almost four months, Rehmat didn't speak to anyone. She spent those four months locked inside her small room. Those four months felt like four years to her. She was waiting, but even more difficult than waiting was passing the time. She would often start crying while sitting alone. She would stop eating in the middle of a meal. Sometimes, she even stopped talking to her family. Somehow, she managed to get through those four months, but even after that, there was no call from Raaz. One day, she made a request to her mother—one that, if it had been anyone else, they might have slapped her for saying it. Rehmat asked her mother to buy a bungalow in Muzaffarnagar—right next to Raaz's house. Hearing this, her mother was stunned for a few moments. She then asked, "Why do you want to buy a bungalow in Muzaffarnagar specifically?"

Rehmat said, "Because if I live in Muzaffarnagar, I will feel good. It will feel like I am close to Raaz, in his city. He may not meet me, and that's okay, but in that city, I will surely run into him someday. And if he sees me, he will never be able to ignore me." For her mother, fulfilling this request was extremely difficult because she was the sole earner in the family. And Rehmat's request was worth eight to nine crores, an amount that was truly enormous for her mother. At that moment, her mother did not give Rehmat any response. Seeing this, Rehmat felt a bit disheartened.

17

A Hope

A few days later

(Mother took Rehmat to Muzaffarnagar, and the car stopped in front of an old bungalow. She asked, "How do you like your new home?" Rehmat was stunned upon hearing this. She couldn't comprehend what had suddenly happened. The bungalow was very close to Raaz's house. After many days, a sparkle returned to Rehmat's eyes. Happiness had finally returned to her life. For the past six months, Rehmat had been filled with despair and hopelessness, but now, deep inside, she was beaming with joy. She had no idea how hard her mother had worked day and night to buy that bungalow. But a mother could go to any extent for her daughter's happiness.)

I was living in my dream world in Raaz's city. A few days later, I joined a gym, where I met Raaz's friend. He spoke to me very kindly and then asked, "Is Raaz still in your life?"

> *"Maine us shaks ka milna har ek se btaya tha,*
> *Aur ab bichhdna har ek se chhupa rahi thi."*

I confidently and proudly replied, where will Raaz go leaving me? He will always be with me. He asked me for coffee and said, "I'm waiting for you outside. Hearing this, Rehmat deliberately spent four hours at the gym so that he would leave, as she did not feel comfortable talking to this friend at all. Talking to Raaz's friend or going out with him without Raaz felt like a violation of her principles. Seeing this, the friend couldn't wait forever and eventually left. The very next day, I quit that gym as well. Wherever I went, I always met one of Raaz's friends. Seeing them only reminded me of Raaz, and I felt extremely dejected at the gym. For this reason, I stopped going to the gym altogether. He was not with me, yet something or the other related to him always found its way back to me, keeping me from forgetting him.

If you truly desire something with all your heart, the universe makes it possible.

(Finally, Raaz's call came. Seeing his name on the screen, Rehmat was overjoyed. But from the other end, a sharp and stern voice asked that "Why have you come to Muzaffarnagar? What is your purpose? What do you want? Why don't you stop following me? Rehmat, with all the love in her heart, tried to explain - I am not here for any purpose. Our family moved here due to some work. I do not wish any harm upon you. After being away from you, I realized how deeply I love you. Whatever misunderstandings exist, tell me, and I will apologize. I will bring you every happiness in the world. When no one else was there, I was with you, and I still am—and always will be. But Raaz, please come back into my life. Don't leave me alone in this dark time. You have the entire world, but for me, you are my world. Whatever you say, I will accept. I just need your 'yes' and I will handle everything else.

I need only your 'yes' and we will be very happy together. Hearing this, Raaz gave her an ultimatum- You must choose—your dreams or me. Without hesitation, I chose Raaz. But then he made another demand.

(Rehmat, if you want to be with me, you must give up your acting, your photoshoots—everything. Burn your ambitions.)

Nobody knew what kind of love this was of both. For the first time, Raaz saw Rehmat completely surrendering herself, begging only for his love, while Raaz was setting fire to everything that made her happy. He didn't even consider her feelings. Yet, even on that day, Rehmat agreed to his impossible demand. Raaz was left stunned— he never thought Rehmat would ever give up her dreams for him. But when he realized she was unbreakable, he executed the plan he had set in motion long before. He had made Rehmat's biggest enemy his closest friend and had already invited him to Canada months ago. Rehmat had no idea, but Raaz deliberately revealed this to her and said, from now on, I will be with him. Hearing this, she shattered even more, as if a dagger had been plunged into her heart. On top of that, the cats (Kalo and Majju) that he had given her still wandered around her, reminding her of him.

After Raaz left, Rehmat cut off all ties with his friends. She believed that all of them belonged to Raaz, and when Raaz himself was gone, she had no reason to stay connected with anyone. She had always cared more about Raaz's reputation than her own. But after he left, many of his friends—and even some of his enemies—tried to talk to her.

"Itni haseen, itne paise wale chehre mile, magar tum nhi mile
Kuch to bilkul uske jese bhi mile magar tum nhi mile shayri,
Mehfil aur tumhari pasandida biryani bhi, milne ke ishare mile
Mahgar tum nhi mile"

On the other hand, Raaz had left no stone unturned in breaking Rehmat. The enemy she once feared had now become Raaz's closest ally—stronger than ever. Despite everything, Rehmat's eyes were filled with tears, yet her love for him remained. She only said one thing-No matter what you did, forget it. I forgive you."

Hearing this, Raaz thought Rehmat would finally give up on him. But she didn't. So, Raaz lashed out at her again. Listen, my engagement is fixed. She is a Muslim girl. I am getting married very soon. We have no future together.

"Wo jate waqt hazar galtiya ginwa gya,
Main soch rahi thi ki jab hum mile the
Toh kya hunar dekha hoga usne mujhme"

Stop following me. Stay away from me. I am fed up with you. I am very happy with someone else. I don't need you anymore. I have sworn on my parents that I will never have anything to do with you again. Saying this, he cut the call and blocked her number. Rehmat broke down. Because this Muzaffarnagar bungalow was her last attempt to show how much she loved him. She tried calling Raaz from ten different numbers, but one by one, he blocked them all. She couldn't believe that this was the same Raaz who once loved her like a mother.

> *"Ro raha tha dil mera aur ankhen bhi*
> *meri Rooh tak rula gya tha vo shaks*
> *Jo mujhse kehta tha ki*
> *'ro mat tere rone se mujhe rona aata hai'"*

This was the same Raaz who had promised to stay with her forever. It was incredibly difficult for her to believe. For the first time, she had lowered herself for someone, and she never imagined Raaz would humiliate her so much that she would regret being alive.

> *"Ki wo ek hi shaks samajhta tha use,*
> *fir yu hua ki wo bhi waqt rehte bahut samjhdar ho gya."*

On one side, Raaz was drifting further away from her with each passing day. On the other side, (the cats) Majju and Kalo would run away from home every day. The helpless Rehmat, devastated by life, would walk miles—into unfamiliar cities—like a madwoman, searching for Majju and Kalo. She would eventually bring them back home, then sit and stare at them with teary eyes for hours. Sometimes, Rehmat would ask strangers on the street for their phones, recharge their numbers with her own money, and call Raaz. But the moment he heard her say "Hello," he would blacklist her. It was never about religion, parents, the future, or faith. The truth was, someone else had entered Raaz's life, and because of that, he now wanted to get rid of Rehmat.

18

Begging for Love

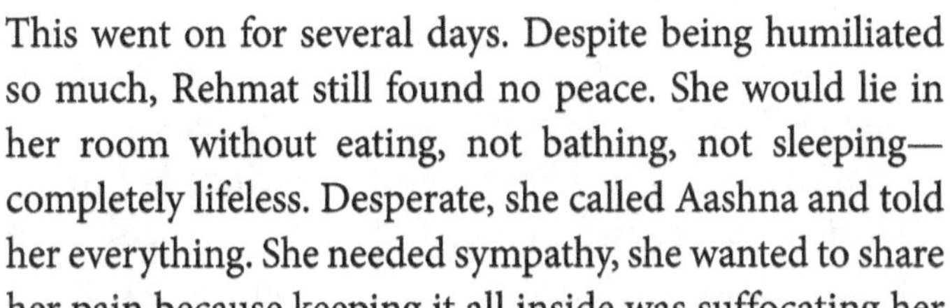

This went on for several days. Despite being humiliated so much, Rehmat still found no peace. She would lie in her room without eating, not bathing, not sleeping—completely lifeless. Desperate, she called Aashna and told her everything. She needed sympathy, she wanted to share her pain because keeping it all inside was suffocating her day by day.

Kehte hai, "Na dosti badi na pyar bada,
Jo nibha de wo shaks bada."

But here, love had already kicked her down, and friendship had shattered the little courage she had left. Even Aashna stopped picking up her calls because she had made new friends at college, friends with whom she went out and had fun. In that world of enjoyment, why would anyone want to talk to a broken soul? Even Aashna abandoned her in this difficult time. Rehmat's condition worsened with each passing day. The shock of Raaz leaving had struck her hard. She had become a living corpse, spending every moment thinking about him. One day, her phone rang. When she picked it up, she saw it was Raaz. Her heart leaped with joy. It was a video call. The moment Rehmat saw Raaz, her eyes welled up with tears.

Once again, she stretched out her hands, begging for love. But Raaz crushed her heart into pieces all over again. Rehmat folded her hands before him, she pleaded, but Raaz showed no mercy. She even said, "Please don't block me. I won't disturb you again. I won't call or message you. Live your life without talking to me.

But what if I don't get your support, your feeling is enough for me. The moment she said that, Raaz instantly blocked her. It felt as if Raaz enjoyed watching her suffer. He had no concern left in him. Every day, he would video call her just to watch her beg and cry, only to block her again. He was taking his revenge, and in some twisted way, her misery satisfied him. Rehmat had completely forgotten who she was—she had become nothing but a puppet in his hands. At that moment, if Raaz had told her to bring the moon, she would have done everything in her power to try.

> *"Na jane kaise us shaks ne chhup ke, chupke se sab kuch badla*
> *Chehra badla, rasta badla, rang badla,*
> *baad me niyat badli aur fir thikana badla*
> *Are mai to duniya se yeh kahti thi,*
> *Mera naam badal dena agar wo shaks badla"*

Muzaffarnagar, its people, its mansion, and its surroundings were slowly consuming her. Raaz's changed behavior had hollowed her out from inside. I used to run barefoot to fulfill his every need. But when it was my turn, his whole world drowned. She had no sense of time, no awareness of herself. The only thing that occupied her mind—day and night—was Raaz. The same Raaz who once claimed to love her more than life itself was now the one determined to destroy her. It was hard to believe, but after he left, Rehmat realized just how much she truly loved him.

He always called me his love, but it took me forever to understand the difference between saying 'you love someone' and actually loving them. Because the truth was—Rehmat loved him. But Raaz was only ever good at saying the words.

For the first time in her life, she understood that grief kills everything—hunger, thirst, time, sleep. Out of the 24 hours in a day, 20 were spent thinking about Raaz, and the remaining four were filled with dreams of him.

"Mujhe usse mile huye ek arsa hua tha aur baat kare kayi din,
Use karib se dekhe ek arsa hua tha aur itminan se sune kayi din
Din chhod, raat chhod, subah bhi chhod, sham bhi chhod, har waqt
tera intzar kiya maine
Uska hath padke kayi din guzar gye, aisa mehsus kiye arsa hua
"Kabhi kabhi to mai neend se uthkar idhar udhar dhundhne lagti
thi itne karib aa jata tha vo mere"
Wo shaks meri din, raat, subah, sham har waqt me sma gya tha
aur mera dil bhi beyiman ho gya tha
Yeh dhatkta toh mere liye tha magar tadpta uske liye"

Even in dreams, she would hold onto him tightly, knowing that he would leave her again. If she couldn't have Raaz, then at least his memories would be enough to keep her alive. She had once clicked a picture of him. Now, that picture was pulling her into its depths. She would spend entire days staring at it. She wanted to cry until she could cry no more, she wanted to scream, she wanted to shout—but only in front of Raaz. Because for her, no one else in the world mattered. The desperation to have him back had consumed all other desires. Days of not bathing led to fungus in her hair, causing it to fall out. Excessive crying made her eyes burn, and dark circles formed around them. She was constantly exhausted, weak, and suffered from severe headaches and restlessness.

> *"Jeena haram kar rkha tha meri in ankho ne khulte hi*
> *Nikal jati thi teri safar – a - talash me aur band hote*
> *Hi nikal jati thi tere safar–a–khwab me"*

A time came when she started seeing Raaz. Sometimes, she felt like he was sitting beside her, and she would talk to him endlessly. Other times, she imagined him watching her from afar. There were moments when she even saw Raaz's face in the people around her—mistaking her own family members for him and speaking to them as if they were Raaz.

Her mother watched in agony as Rehmat locked herself away in a room, slipping further into madness with each passing day. Rehmat's obsession with Raaz grew worse, consuming her completely. Anyone who tried to stop her from meeting Raaz became her enemy—including her own mother. Her mother desperately tried to bring her back to reality. But Rehmat saw anyone who said, "Raaz is not here," as a liar. Her mother's words felt unbearable, and she would scream at her, fight with her. For Rehmat, her mother had become the biggest villain of her life. One day, after a terrible fight, Rehmat decided to leave home. She grabbed all her clothes and got into the car. But her hands were trembling. She was too weak to even insert the key properly. There was no strength left in her body. She had made up her mind to leave but where would she even go? Just then, her mother stepped in front of the car, blocking her way. Rehmat told her to move, but she wouldn't budge. Rehmat assumed that if she moved the car forward, her mother would step aside. But she didn't. Rehmat lost control of the steering, and her mother fell. The household staff rushed to pick her up and rushed her to the hospital. Her condition was serious. There were no external injuries, but she had suffered a heart attack. She remained in the hospital for nine days. Shame and guilt consumed Rehmat.

It took ten days for her mother to fully regain consciousness. The first thing she asked when she woke up was—"Are you still planning to leave home?" Hearing this, Rehmat burst into tears. Unknowingly, she had made a terrible mistake—one she deserved to be punished for. But instead of punishment, her mother placed a hand on her head and pulled her into a tight embrace. They returned home together. At her mother's request, Rehmat tried to gather herself again. But just four days into her attempt.

19

Moonlit Night

One day, Raaz called again, and for some reason, he seemed extremely distressed and dejected. The first thing he did was apologize for all his mistakes.

(He told Rehmat that he was coming back because he wasn't happy in Canada and that he wanted to stay with her. Hearing this, she couldn't contain her joy and was overwhelmed with happiness. However, Raaz gave her one condition—that no one should know about his return. Rehmat, anxiously waiting for him, felt every hour passing like a year. Days went by in this anticipation. Then, one day, suddenly, the doorbell rang. When she opened the door, the sight before her left her speechless. Raaz was standing right there. A gust of wind passed through her hair as she stood frozen in shock. He had brought a large black bag and a blanket with him—the very blanket Rehmat had given him, her favorite one. Why had he brought that blanket with him?)

Tears welled up in my eyes at the sight of him. People see the world with both their eyes, but I had seen my entire world within his eyes. The first thing he did was pull me into his arms. I had prepared a long list of grievances, but with that embrace, he erased all my complaints. At that moment, I felt as if God had returned all my lost happiness to me. I quickly took him to meet my mother. She was delighted to see him too. But his eyes were strangely moist, and he kept apologizing to me over and over again. My world had started revolving around him once again. I had forgotten every pain he had given me because now, I never wanted to lose him again. After his return, my life took a beautiful turn. He became the remedy for all my ailments, the cure for all my sorrows. He cared for me as if I were the most delicate thing in the world. Every difficulty I faced now became his problem to solve. Once again, I was his "Chapri," and he was my "Maju"—a name I had lovingly given him. Happiness had returned to our home. He started taking care of me like before—pampering me, feeding me, staying with me all day. In the evenings, he would even practice shooting with me. His aim was always perfect, while mine was always crooked. Whenever I missed a shot, he would laugh heartily, and when I pouted in frustration, he would gently wipe my tears, take my hands in his, and teach me how to aim properly. Whenever he went out, he would bring back salwar suits for me, make me try them on, and exclaim, "Wow, you look beautiful!" But in truth, it wasn't me who was beautiful; it was his heart. Because even though he had once shattered me, he had now pieced me back together in such a way that no power in the world could separate us again. Days passed, and life with Raaz was once again filled with joy. For him, I had started learning how to cook, something I had never liked before. I wanted to prepare his favorite dish—biryani—with my own hands. Though I was a vegetarian and hated even the sight of eggs, for Raaz, I was willing to do anything. I sent my driver to buy chicken and then went to the kitchen, where my mother was already present. She asked me what was in the black bag. I told her that Raaz loved biryani, and today I was going to cook it for him. Saying this, I started washing the meat. But suddenly, my mother held my hands, washed them, and took me outside to the car. She instructed the driver to take us to Delhi. (All along the way, I kept asking my mother where we were going, but she didn't answer even once. Raaz was sitting in the front seat with the driver. I asked him too, but he, like my mother, remained silent. The car finally stopped in front of a hospital. My mother took an emergency appointment and led me inside. Rehmat was left sitting outside with Raaz, utterly confused about what was happening.)

After a while, my mother called me in. The doctor asked me just one question: "Who is Raaz?" I immediately called for him and said, "Doctor, he's calling you. Come inside, Raaz." Raaz entered the room. The doctor asked me again, "Who is Raaz?" I replied, "The person standing right in front of you is Raaz. "The doctor said, "Rehmat, apart from you, me, and your mother, there is no one else in this room." His absurd joke infuriated me. I turned to Raaz and smiled at him. Then I asked my mother, "Why are we here?" The doctor replied, "Rehmat, you have a condition called hallucination. It is a disorder where a person can see, hear, touch, and even talk to someone who isn't actually present. This condition makes you believe that the person exists when, in reality, they do not."

(The doctor's words shook me to the core. I turned to Raaz and begged him to speak to the doctor and prove that he wasn't just a hallucination. But he remained silent, watching everything unfold as if he were a spectator. I fell to my knees, pleading with him, desperate to prove to everyone that Raaz was real, that he was with me.)

I clutched his feet, but he couldn't give any proof of his existence. He just stood there, smiling like a lifeless statue.

Ek bar fir mera dil tuta
Ek bar fir uska sath chhuta
Ek bar fir wo mujhse rutha
Ek bar fir mera sab luta

(Like water slipping through fingers, I crumbled. Tears flowed from my eyes like a waterfall. I stood before him, hands folded, pleading. The shock was too much for me to bear, and I collapsed. When I woke up, I was told that I had been unconscious for five days. The trauma had been so severe that I had gone into a coma for five days. When I opened my eyes, my entire family was standing in front of me, their eyes filled with the desperate hope that I would recover. But even amidst them, I could still see Raaz, silently standing there, looking at me.)

Due to hallucinations, my mental stability had severely deteriorated. The doctors prescribed heavy medication to suppress my thoughts, making it difficult for me to think or feel anything clearly. I spent most of my days asleep because of those medicines. They were effectively erasing Raaz from my real life, but as soon as I closed my eyes, he would invade my dreams.

"Mujhe dhundh leti thi uski yaad har ek bahane se, uski
Yaad wakif thi mere har ek thikane se"

I often found myself crying in my dreams, begging Raaz not to leave. The dreams tormented me so much that I would wake up in shock, unable to sleep for the rest of the night. I couldn't believe that Raaz was not with me. When the medication took effect, I would feel numb, forgetting everything. But as soon as I slept, Raaz would return. My life had lost all its colors. I could no longer tell whether I was alive or dead. The medications made me gain weight, my body weakened, and even lifting a glass of water became an ordeal.

(Unable to bear it anymore, I made a decision—to end my life. There were over a hundred pills in the house. I gathered them all and swallowed as many as I could. And then—when I opened my eyes again, I was in a hospital, once more. My entire family stood before me, their heads bowed in sorrow. My little brother was there too, tears streaming down his innocent face. He held my hand and said in a trembling voice, "Look, I'll give you all my toys. I'll even get you your favorite cake. Just promise me you'll never do this again.")

I had begged Raaz for love, but now, my family was begging me for my life. In this vast world, I don't know why he crossed my path. He neither let me live nor let me die. I was standing at the edge of life—behind me was a deep pit, in front of me a deep well. And I was trapped in between.

20

An Attempt for a New Beginning

(To overcome this hesitation, Rehmat's mother made a big decision for her. She knew that if she left Rehmat alone this time, she might lose her forever. She also understood that to remove Raaz from Rehmat's heart, someone else had to take his place. No matter how much she thought about it, Raaziv seemed to be the best choice. So, she approached Raaziv's family and asked for Rehmat's hand in marriage. Raaziv's family had always liked Rehmat and happily accepted her. For Raaziv, it felt like a long-cherished dream coming true. But Rehmat was still stuck on Raaz somewhere in her heart. When her mother proposed the match, Rehmat once again rejected Raaziv. Until now, only she had been troubled, but now, because of her, two families were distressed. The strong bond between both families was damaged. But at that moment, her mother cared less about family ties and more about saving her daughter's life. She lovingly explained to Rehmat that she needed to move on from the dream life she had imagined with Raaz. It wouldn't be easy, but with effort, everything would fall into place. However, Rehmat kept resisting every attempt her mother made. This time, her mother made her swear—saying that she had already done enough of what she wanted, but now, she would have to listen to her.)

Her mother brought another proposal. This time, the man belonged to their own community. His name was Veer. Veer was the nephew of a prominent minister and a successful businessman. He owned ten clubs in Delhi and was well-known in elite circles. Veer had always desired a beautiful bride, and he saw that beauty in Rehmat. In fact, he had first seen her five years ago at a wedding. Back then, his family had sent a proposal, but since Rehmat was too young at the time, the matter didn't proceed further.

When I first saw Veer, I immediately found flaws in him. The truth was, I found flaws in every face I looked at—perhaps because my eyes had trained themselves to see only imperfections. I composed myself and, remembering my mother's words, forced myself to look at Veer again. But the moment I did, memories of my past flooded back. To be honest, I wasn't happy. This was just a compulsion—I had no real desire to move forward with Veer. So, I told him about Raaz, hoping he would back out of this relationship himself. After hearing everything, he asked me only one question—

"Is he still a part of your life today?"

"He is not in my life anymore, but I still think about him a lot, and I am deeply troubled." Veer replied, "So what? Everyone has a past. I don't care about your past; I care about your present. I will always stand by you and take care of you. And if you're troubled, I'll find a solution for your problems. If I succeed, great. If not, then we'll face the troubles together."

Rehmat's Inner Struggle & Veer's Persistence

Hearing this, I smiled. I had shared Raaz's story hoping it would end this relationship, but things turned out differently. Veer was a good man—level-headed and, most importantly, understanding. Maybe I should have given him a chance.

I liked meeting him, but I still wasn't ready to replace Raaz with anyone else. Yet, Veer was relentless. He put in every ounce of effort to win me over. I had no idea what he saw in me that made him so determined.

He did everything I liked. Sometimes, he would come over and cook my favorite food, but I never ate from his hands. Every time he tore a bite and extended it toward me, I saw Raaz instead. Sometimes, he left all his work just to sit with me, reciting poetry or cracking jokes. His jokes never made me laugh, but for his sake, I smiled— and he would record that laughter and set it as his phone's ringtone.Whenever he came to meet me, he brought a car full of white roses. He introduced me to all his friends and gave me a grand welcome at his club. Three female bodyguards always accompanied me, which I didn't like at all. I couldn't even count how many of his principles he had broken just to make me happy.

Veer knew everything about my past, yet he walked beside me without hesitation. He would bring diamond rings, wedding bangles, gold earrings—once, he even had my name engraved on his car's windshield and beamed with joy.

But accepting such expensive gifts before marriage didn't sit right with me. Besides, they didn't bring me any real happiness. A month passed like this, and in that time, he taught me a lot—how to visit a temple, how to eat on time, how to sleep on time. I was trying to forget Raaz, bit by bit. I had always wanted to start a business, and within just two days, Veer involved me in his own business so my mind could focus on work instead of wandering aimlessly. Now, he was becoming the relief for all my wounds. I was genuinely trying to remove Raaz from my heart, but his memories still lingered. They weighed on my sleep. Every night, I found myself lying awake, lost in thoughts of him. In the middle of the night, I would wake up and think about him again. Veer had put his heart and soul into winning me over. Sometimes, when he held my hand, Raaz's face would immediately flash before my eyes, and I would pull my hand away.

"Aisa nhi tha ki meri nazar kabhi kisi aur se mili nhi,
Magar usse jo mili thi nazar
Fir meri yeh nazre kahi aur uthi nhi"

These emotions, these memories, were turning into an invisible wall between us.

(But Veer had immense faith in his love. He believed that one day, I would realize just how much he loved me.

21

The Labyrinth

Veer was ready to do anything for me, with all his heart and soul. But fate had something else in store for me. Once again, my phone rang. When I picked it up, a familiar voice asked, "How are you?" How could I tell him my true condition? After all, he had never seen me after sunset.

It was Raaz. The same person who had once abandoned me to die. My past stood before me once again. He wanted to meet me one last time. He kept asking, but I made excuses or ignored him every time. Perhaps, deep down, he had finally realized that what he did to me was wrong. I didn't want Raaz to return because Veer was now in my life—and I did not want to betray him. For four or five days, Raaz tried hard to convince me. I even blacklisted his number. But he kept calling me from different numbers. How long could I keep my heart cold? Finally, I decided to meet him one last time, out of basic human decency—especially since he had come all the way back from Canada. Without telling Veer, I gathered my courage and went to meet Raaz. My eyes sparkled with anticipation. I knew Veer was in my life now, but somewhere deep inside, Raaz still had a place in my heart. My heart was racing.

I wore an old black shirt and pajama, while he showed up in an elegant pant and shirt. He looked like a dream—so much so that I started wondering if I was hallucinating. He ordered two pastries for me and one for himself. As he sat in front of me, a familiar sense of anxiety and unease started creeping in. Before he could even ask, "How are you?" a wave of pain surged in my chest. He had shattered me so much that my soul trembled at the sight of him. I felt as if he had come back to kill me this time, to completely destroy me.

I immediately told him I needed to leave. A thousand questions swirled in my mind, but I couldn't bring myself to stay.Before he could say anything else, I hurriedly left and made my way home. As soon as I reached, I took medicine to calm my mind and went to sleep without telling anyone what had happened. The next morning, I woke up to nearly a hundred missed calls from Raaz. I blocked every number he had tried to reach me from. I had no other choice—I was more worried about Veer than myself.

If I took even a single step towards Raaz, it would mean betraying Veer. So, while Raaz was in Muzaffarnagar, I left Muzaffarnagar. I didn't want to breathe the same air that had touched Raaz and reached me. Even after I left, he continued calling me from different numbers. It wasn't that Raaz had completely left my heart, but every time I thought about him, all I could remember was how he had left me suffering in the middle of my journey—how he had indulged in a life of pleasure, got a new girlfriend, befriended my enemies, smiled while I begged for him, how I had seizures, how my hallucinations still haunted me, how I had been mentally destroyed. And now, he had come back—perhaps to send me to my final destination, to end me for good. After many failed attempts to reach me, Raaz finally gave up and returned to Canada.

Almost ten months had passed with Veer. Now, the discussion had turned to setting a wedding date. I was happy, thinking that Veer would now take care of everything. I was trying to move forward in my life. So many months had passed, yet I still hadn't been able to completely move on with Veer. Even at that moment, I was just trying.

"Na jane us shaks ko kaun sa hunar aata tha
Raat hoye hi jehan me utar aata tha
Mai uski yaado se niklne ki koshish me thi
Lekin wo mere zindagi ke har raste pr khda nazar aata
tha"

All the wedding preparations were done, but my heart wasn't fully ready for this marriage. Veer loved me in every possible way, but despite all his affection, he could never take Raaz's place. Or perhaps, I simply didn't want to give him that place. He loved me like Raaz did—there was love, passion, and a deep sense of belonging. Nothing was missing in him... except that he was not Raaz.

One day, during a casual conversation, a fight broke out between me and Veer, and in the heat of the moment, I compared him to Raaz. That struck Veer deeply. He folded his hands and pleaded with me never to utter that name again. I realized my mistake, but by then, Raaz had started haunting my thoughts again, day after day. Because of this, I began searching for Raaz in Veer. But I couldn't find even the slightest trace of him. This led to constant arguments between Veer and me. He had begun to understand why I was behaving this way. He knew that Raaz was still alive in my heart.

<h1 style="text-align:center">22</h1>

<h1 style="text-align:center">The Final Stage of Humiliation</h1>

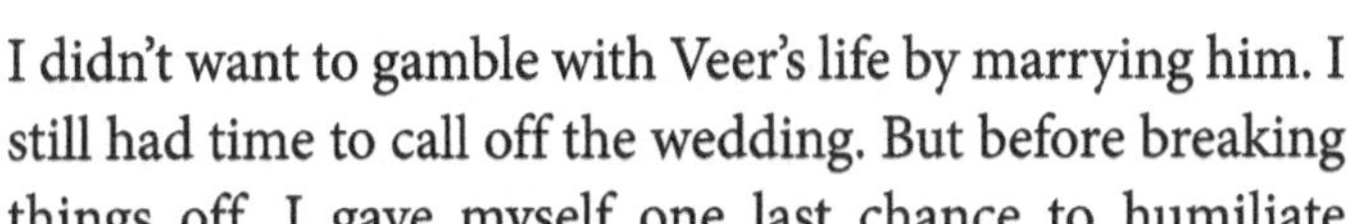

I didn't want to gamble with Veer's life by marrying him. I still had time to call off the wedding. But before breaking things off, I gave myself one last chance to humiliate myself—by reaching out to Raaz.

It was around 2 AM. I had been thinking about Raaz for a long time, wanting to ask him where exactly he had left me stranded. I had always punished myself for his mistakes, but now, in a way, even Veer was suffering because of them. After hours of crying, thinking, and pulling myself together, I finally called Raaz. My hands had gone cold, and my eyes were filled with tears. I wanted to ask him one last time—should I really move on? He answered the call. As soon as he said "Hello," I forgot everything I had planned to say. Suddenly, all those moments I had struggled to escape came rushing back. I had meant to ask him something else, but instead, I blurted out, "Raaz, you gave me a watch once... take it back."I knew how absurd that sounded, but the moment those words left my mouth, tears streamed down my face, and I broke down, sobbing uncontrollably. I wanted Raaz to ask me what was wrong. Instead, he got angry—again. He insulted me, threw a slur at me, one that was directed at my mother. And then, once more, he put me in my place—by hanging up the call.

The irony? I had already returned that watch to him three years ago. I cried the whole night. Veer kept calling me all morning, but I didn't pick up. I spent the entire day drowning in my sorrow. By evening, Veer came to see me. Seeing my condition, he kept asking why I was crying. After three and a half hours, I finally broke down and told him everything about the night before. Veer listened carefully. He didn't just hear me—he understood me. And then, he too broke down. In the end, he asked me just one question: "What was missing in my love?" I had no answer. That night, he took care of me. He fed me, placed cold compresses on my forehead—I had a fever of 103 degrees. Then, he sat with my family and cracked jokes as if nothing had happened. But when I looked into his eyes, I saw his pain." That day, he promised me that no matter what happens, he will never leave me in my bad times."

At that moment, I felt ashamed of myself. Why was I playing with the heart of this beautiful, selfless man? Raaz had destroyed me, and now, no one seemed enough for me anymore. He had become my ultimate defeat—after him, I had no desire to win anything.

But I refused to ruin Veer's life the way mine had been ruined. That very day, I decided to push Veer away. I lovingly told him, "I'm not ready for marriage right now." Without hesitation, he replied, "I will wait for you. "I knew getting him to walk away wouldn't be easy.

So, to make him leave me, I demanded that he buy me a 2,000-square-yard mansion and put four famous clubs under my name—within a month. I knew he had money, but not enough to fulfill such demands in such a short time. I thought this would finally break him. But astonishingly, even after hearing my conditions, he didn't back down. He used up all his savings. He even pawned his gold bracelet to buy the mansion in Delhi. Every morning, he took me around the city, searching for land. My heart was in dilemma because, deep down, I wanted none of it. I just wanted him to give up, to step away from this madness, to refuse to marry me. But he didn't. He found the land. And just before he could deposit the token money—

I sat with my family and called off the wedding.

Hearing this, my mother nearly fainted. She was exhausted—exhausted from dealing with me. But I was doing what I believed was right. Once again, both our families gathered, and the decision was made to officially break the engagement. It was humiliating. Veer's family was insulted. Ours was, too. When Veer found out, he insisted on meeting me one last time. He had lost his mind. He slapped himself 20-25 times. A madness had taken over him—I had never seen this side of him before. It terrified me. His eyes were bloodshot, his ears red, and despite sitting in an air-conditioned car, he was sweating profusely. Then, he broke down in tears. Watching him like that, I hated myself. How many people was I going to hurt—just for the sake of one man? As I was lost in these thoughts, Veer suddenly asked, "You're doing all of this for Raaz, aren't you? He's still in your heart, isn't he?" I immediately denied it. And then, Veer told me something—Something I was completely unprepared to hear.

23

Illusion

Through his tears, Veer said to me, "The man for whom you have ruined so many lives was never truly yours. He told me everything himself—every little thing about you. Your madness for him, your every action… If you hear what I know, you'll hate yourself. He never loved you. He only wanted revenge for the humiliation you caused him, but he never got to finish what he started. Behind your back, he roamed around with his ex-lovers, posting pictures while holding their hands. What you called love was nothing but vengeance."

Hearing this, I exploded in anger. I lashed out at Veer, saying, "No matter what, Raaz would never speak ill of me. I know him better than anyone. If something about me bothered him, he would tell me, not badmouth me to others. I swear on my life—he would never betray me. And I will always stand by him, just as I have before, and always will. No one can ever replace Raaz, and I won't let anyone try."I had taken every accusation against Raaz upon myself.

That day, something inside me broke loose, something I had kept bottled up for a long time. I had wronged Veer in the worst way at the very last turn of our relationship.

I never intended to leave him like that, but I stormed off, leaving him in tears and rage. Yet that night, I realized once again—Raaz was still alive inside me. The next day, Veer came to my house for one final discussion. In front of everyone, he asked, "Will you move forward in life with me? I have forgiven all your mistakes. I still love you."

I was shocked—and ashamed. How could someone still make space for me in their heart after everything I had done? I returned all the expensive gifts he had given me. He refused to take them, but I no longer had the right to keep them. Before leaving, Veer said one last thing:" I know you're doing all this for him. But remember this— the man you are fighting the world for does not respect you. I spoke to Raaz myself. In his version of the story, you are nothing but a greedy woman. He told me you make a habit of trapping new men every day. He even claimed that you took a loan of Rs.10,00,000 from him and never paid it back. He told me about police cases, the car you took as a gift—he said you treated him like a driver and only used him. That car? He said you got it just for yourself. He tried to ruin your image in my eyes. He called you a toy, something to be played with. He twisted every fact against you. That man is not worthy of you. By the time you realize this, I will be long gone. I loved you deeply. I dreamt of marrying you. But I will always regret that I could never find a place in your heart."

I didn't believe anything Veer said—I was sure he was lying just to make me hate Raaz. So I paid no attention to his words and dismissed them completely. But after Veer left, I fell into depression again. The hallucinations I had once overcome—ones Veer had helped me fight—began creeping back.

I withdrew into myself. Rajeev tried talking to me, but I was so lost in my suffering that the whole world seemed pointless. After several failed attempts, one day, Rajeev finally got me to talk. He asked how I was. I had shattered completely, unable to control myself, and I told him everything. Hearing my pain, Rajeev became deeply disturbed. At a time when no one else stood by me, he did. He encouraged me day and night to move forward. He reminded me of my worth—who I was. He couldn't be my life partner, but he was always my friend. Every time I needed him, he was there. But maybe I never truly saw him—perhaps I never wanted to, because in my eyes, no one could compare to Raaz. I asked Rajeev, "Veer is gone, but the things he said about Raaz—could they be true?" This question haunted me day and night.

Days passed. And then, one day, Rehmat's patience broke. She turned to her mother and said, "Please, just once, call Raaz and ask him if he really said all that about me." Her mother knew that Rehmat was suffering. Though reluctant, she dialed Raaz's number.

She believed that no matter what, Raaz would never speak ill of Rehmat to anyone else. He might have said things directly to her, but he would never allow a third person to insult her. But when Raaz answered, everything shattered. He did not deny a single accusation. He shamelessly confirmed every single thing Veer had told me. It was hard to believe how low he had sunk. The man who once played the role of a devoted lover had been scheming behind my back all along.

Then he said something even more shocking."Rehmat should have had the sense not to discuss me with her future husband. But now that Veer is gone, I have a suggestion, Aunty—why don't you just marry her off to Rajeev? He's been waiting for her long enough anyway."

24

No Desire

In this world, justice is served on paper, but I had already accepted my fate in his eyes. He knew about my destruction, and yet, he turned away from me as if he knew nothing. No one can break a woman, but a cowardly man, by playing the game of love, can make her fall face-first into the ground.

Even today, my sleep is upset with me. I told it, "He has left—the one I used to stay awake for at night," but now, sleep refuses to recognize me.

Aisi koi dargah nhi, mandir nhi
Jaha tujhe manga nhi
Eh khuda tu deta kyu ni aakhir maine kon si tujhse
Jannat mang li?
Khuda- Jinse tujhe chaha nahi, manga nahi
Tum use mil jao, yeh insaf toh nhi

My mother told me some paths in life are of patience, and some are lessons. Filling my hands with patience, I went to my God once again, folded my hands, and begged to forget you. But as soon as I touched my forehead in prayer, I ended up asking for you again. I still hadn't learned my lesson. Perhaps, I was meant to be humiliated even more.

He called me greedy in front of everyone. If only I hadn't sold my jewelry that day, if only I hadn't taken that car for him, perhaps he would've given me a better name. I abandoned the world for him, and now, I look around—there is no one in sight.

Perhaps, I have been cursed by the very world I set ablaze for him.

Ek tarfa mohabbat hoti toh baat alag hoti masla
Is baat ka hai jab nazre miti thi toh muskuraya wo
Bhi tha.

Waada "aakhir tak" ka kiya tha,
wo jatata bahut tha
Magar nibhana bhul gya,
Uski tasvire ko kuch aise smbhal ke rkha hai maine
Jaise yeh meri umar bhar ki kmayi ho.
Mera maksad use pane ka kbhi nhi tha
Waada umar bhar chahne ka tha sirf.

Haan ye baat sach hai ki kisi ke bina koi marta nhi
Bas insan jina bhul jata hai
Har chij berang si lagti hai
Shayar nahi sirf dil mar jata hai
Wah ek shaks chup hai mujhse aur mai chup hu pure Zamane se.

Sometimes, I imagine him in front of me. And then, if by mistake, I actually see him, I don't turn back.

Days pass, but every evening that belonged to him, I still spend alone.

Mai janti hu mai mar chuki hu
Fir bhi mai khud ko zinda dikha rahi hu
Ander se sab bikhar rha hai,
Lekin bahr se sab sawar rahi hu.
Use toh khawabo me mil leti hu lekin
Mai aaj bhi khud ko dhundhne ke liye jgah-jgah
Bhatkati hu.
Daal rkha hai maine apne khuda ko kashmkash me,
Har din tujhe bhulne ki koshish me hu,
har din tujhe Pane ki duao me hu.

I don't know how my life has stopped at this strange crossroad— if I think of you, I can't sleep, and if I sleep, I dream only of you.

Teri jaan ki kasam
Eh meri jaan
Tu yaad na aaye kisi raat,
aisi koi raat nhi.

This world's sympathy feels like poison to me now because I remember how fake consolations destroyed my world. What are you thinking, oh betrayer?

Yes, it's me. Your betrayal even turned me into a poet. I learned to write ghazals through my tears. I don't mention you anywhere anymore, yet people still say, "The one she loved must have been extraordinary."How do I explain to these people? It took me an eternity to turn emotions into words. Not everyone becomes a poet just because their heart is broken.

They say— A woman's loyalty is tested when a man has nothing to offer, and she still chooses him. A man's loyalty is tested when he has everything to offer, and he still chooses the same woman.I believed that I was worthy of your good times because only I was there during your bad times. Everyone else had left you, but in the end, only my love and I remained by your side.

Afsos is baat ka ki teri jatayi mohabbat jhuthi thi,
Teri har ek baat juthi thi, jutha tha ye rishta hmara.
Itni badi sajish karke
Saare gunah karke
Gunahgar bhi mujhe thehra diya,

Don't worry— I never let a single accusation touch you. Because for me, the real issue was your honor, your loyalty. I took the blame upon myself, told everyone— "I failed to keep the relationship."

One day, you'll stand with strangers, and I will pass by, pretending I don't know you. If I had won you, the story would have ended. But you have broken me so uniquely that this story will go on for a lifetime.Whenever people will talk about the past, I will deny you again and again. My heart is foolish, it refuses to accept reality. I asked it last night— "What is our relationship now?" And with pride, it replied, "I don't belong to you anymore. I belong to him."It's okay. This innocent heart will understand someday.

It loved someone who crushed it under his feet. I begged for love, I cried, I pleaded, I suffered, I almost died— and yet, I asked for him from him. And he kicked me away and walked ahead. The strangest part? The shoes he wore when he stepped over me, I still keep them safe in the cupboard of my delusions. That cat you gave me— she still throws tantrums, runs away, and creates havoc. I still care, but I won't ask about you anymore. Maybe you are better in my memories, because I can't bear to see you change.

A few moments with you felt like a dream, but now, I no longer have the obsession to ask fate for you. Even in a crowded gathering, you are the only one I see, but I will never beg for you again. Yes, I am letting you go today, but that doesn't mean you will leave my heart too. Because my heart is innocent— it will someday understand your deception. I remember you, not just in the darkness of the night, but in the brightest of days. Among my favorite people, I still remember you. Listen— after you, I never cared for anyone. Many precious souls came into my life, but after you, I never called anyone "mine." Sometimes, everything inside me cries— except my eyes.

Soch rahi hu, aaj tumhe pura likhu
Ya fir adhura hi chhod du
Jaan bhi likhu, bas itna likhu
Ki khud ko tera aur tujhko mera likhu.

Memories hurt, whether good or bad. The day I escape this ocean of sorrow, break free from your captivity, your betrayal— the first thing I will do is refuse to recognize you. Oh time, stand with me— I will shatter your pride, your arrogance, and walk away. Oh God, now my fate shall be decided from the heavens— I no longer trust the verdicts of this world.

Baat agar sabar ki hai toh-
Le kar liya maine sabar –
ja tujhe mera sabar lage.
Mera dil kar raha hai swal mujhse bar-bar
Aakhir wo shaks puch le ek bar is dil ka hal
Toh yakinan mai faink du sari neend ki goliya,

How do I explain to this naïve heart? It must tread carefully— for he is cruel, he embraces only to tear hearts apart. Even if I set out to search for him, it would be in vain. He is the murderer of my soul. If he had merely been lost, I would have found him. But where he has abandoned me, it will take me a lifetime to return from there.

I have a letter— one you never wrote. And every night, I write its reply. Once again, my heart has taken offense to these words. I am going to calm it down— and tonight, it will take a long time. I wonder— if tonight were my last day, what would he do? And if I no longer existed, what would he do? Perhaps, we will meet again. In another world, in a different city, under new names. And when that happens, ask me my name, and I will ask you how you've been. Once more, I will ask for a promise to stay until the end. And this time, fulfill it.

Fir ek dafa puchungi tumse akhir tk ka sath
Aur tum is baar ise mukammal karna
Ab masla dillagi Aur sajish ka nahi
Ab masla mann ka hai
Ab agar wo khuda bhi ban jaye,
Toh bhi uska sajda na karu.
Six years later...